BITE ME

LUNA WILDER

WANT A FREE BOOK?

Want a free copy of Wolf Lover? It's a steamy, scarred military hero, curvy girl romance! Check it out today here!

I need to quit.

I've been telling myself that every day for the last six months.

I knew as soon as I started working for Hudson as his virtual assistant that this wasn't going to work out.

He's rude, bossy, and a total grouch.

I've only managed to last this long because whenever he starts being a jerk, I sass him right back.

Enough is enough, though. It's time for me to find a new job.

Except when I finally meet him in person to tell him that I quit, he refuses to accept my resignation.

Suddenly, instead of the grumpy jerk that I'm used to, Hudson seems to be trying to be almost...nice.

It must be a trap.

Except he says that it's something else.

Can I trust him when he says that we're fated to be?

If you love bear shifters, fated mates, enemies to lovers, and boss romance books, then Bite Me is for you! One-click today and enjoy!

ONE

Isla

"TODAY IS GOING to be the day. I swear, I really mean it this time," I growl as I read over the newest email from my boss, Hudson. The day has hardly begun, and here I am, dreading the ding of my email I know is coming soon.

My boss never sends just one email.

He's the absolute worst.

I was so excited about this job when I applied, and felt so incredibly lucky when my application was accepted. Working from home was a huge draw for me when looking for jobs, and this one paid better than anything else out there. I knew I could answer emails, talk to clients, and do all the other tasks required of a virtual assistant. Easy peasy.

What I didn't expect, however, was for my boss to be a total jerk face.

"Are you grumbling about your boss again?" my best friend, Hattie, asks, her eyebrow raised suspiciously from where she's sitting at the kitchen table. I glare at her from my spot in our living room.

"He's being his usual *charming* self," I mutter sarcastically. Hattie grins, which does nothing to help my mood. She thinks my dynamic with my boss is endlessly amusing. I can think of a few other words to describe my relationship with Hudson. Namely, frustrating, crazy-making, and almost not worth the money.

"By doing what, exactly? Emailing you a list of what to do this week?" she asks. I almost growl at her. We've had this conversation at least a dozen times by now, but she doesn't seem to get it.

"It's not *what* he's doing; it's *how* he's doing it," I inform her. "Tone matters, you know."

"You sound like an old married couple," she muses.

"Oh my god, never say that again," I groan.

"Well, it's not like you don't provoke him. I think you like ruffling Mr. Snarky's feathers."

"I do not!" I insist. By the look my friend is giving me, she's not buying it.

To be fair, ever since that very first email I received from Hudson, I've basically been begging to be fired.

All the articles I could find about my boss online claimed he was a laid-back loner-type. There wasn't a ton of information, presumably because of the lone wolf status, but nothing I read prepared me for working with Hudson.

He must have graduated from loner to recluse in recent years and with it, forgot all of his manners and people skills. My job is to be the buffer between my boss and his clients, but I'm starting to think I might need a buffer between me and Hudson.

The sound of my email dinging pulls me back into the present, and I frown automatically, like a Pavlovian response. Clicking into the message, I read it through before sighing dramatically and collapsing onto my laptop.

"That's it; I'm quitting," I announce, my voice muffled from where my face is buried into the crook of my elbow. Hattie laughs.

"Where are you going to work instead? You know that no place around here is hiring."

She has a point. That's the main reason why I'm still working as Hudson's assistant. I need this job... at least until I can find something else. *God, please let me find something else.*

I've been looking for a new job for months now but without any luck. If I'm being honest with myself, sometimes I think I'm not trying that hard. Some sick part of me actually... *likes* sparring with Hudson. I'm never bored anyway, but our relationship can't be healthy.

I spend way too much time thinking about him and how to respond to his haughty, rude messages. I spend even more time imagining him opening my emails and reading my clever words. Does he ever smile? Maybe just a hint of a smirk? Do I get under his skin the same way he always gets under mine?

He probably never even gives you a second thought; the little voice in the back of my mind chimes in. Helpful, as always.

I try my best to ignore it.

"Look on the bright side," Hattie says as she comes back into the living room. "Maybe he'll fire you this week."

"If only I could be that lucky," I mumble. My head might agree with that statement, but my confused stomach clenches at the thought of him letting me go. As much as I secretly enjoy our back-and-forth, it might actually break my heart to find out Hudson hates me.

"I'm headed out to my own terrible job. Let's both try to get fired today, huh?" Hattie says sarcastically, making me grin.

"We could go out and celebrate after," I joke, and she laughs.

"Sounds like a plan. I'll text you."

"See you!"

She waves as she heads out the door, and I make my way into the kitchen, tightening my pajama pants as I walk to our stove. I fill the kettle up and turn the stove on, getting my teacup down from the cupboard as I wait for the water to boil. In my head, I'm already crafting the perfect response to Hudson's email.

Dear asshat...

No, that's too mean. Be subtle.

Hudson, thank you for your recent email, you annoying little –

No. Not quite right.

Maybe I should just respond with *BITE ME*. That would get my point across pretty efficiently, I think.

The tea kettle starts to whistle, and I turn off the stove, pouring some water over my teabag.

The most recent email from my boss isn't even the worst I've seen from him, which usually means he's finishing something up. Hudson seems to be the nicest when he's caught up in a big project. I think it's because he's too busy and distracted to put much effort into our exchanges. It gives me time to sharpen my verbal skills and create drafts of email rants I'll probably never send.

Hudson is an artist, a sculptor, to be exact. He's damn good, too, though I would never tell him that. His ego is already too big if you ask me. But there's no denying the man's talent. I might not have ever met Hudson face to face, but I know each of his sculptures inside and out.

I'm still amazed at the time he spends with each piece, the care and thought that goes into carving and creating an image only he can see out of a lump of wet clay. The majority of Hudson's works are pottery related, though the most interesting pieces in his portfolio are the abstract sculptures. They show his soul. Maybe Hudson gives everything to his art, and that's why he's such a jerk in real life.

It boggles my mind how someone can be so creative and direct with their art and yet be a total douche-canoe when it comes to actually communicating with another human being.

But I digress.

Hudson has orders for the next four months already lined up, but he likes to take a few days off between projects. Those are the days he's at peak snarkiness.

My email dings again, making my head throb, and I sigh as I grab my tea and head back to my desk. My office space is tucked away in the corner of our living room. Our apartment is a two-bedroom in a rundown building, but I'm trying to keep a positive attitude. Most days, anyway.

Hattie and I moved here a little over a year ago. We left our parents' houses at eighteen, determined to make it in the big city. Hattie and I didn't last four months before we were out of money and forced to move to this small town nearby for affordable rent.

Maybe I should ask Hudson for a raise. I smirk to myself as I take a seat at my desk.

The newest email is from a potential client. I scan it, checking out Hudson's calendar and making a note of his earliest available date. Then I pull up Hudson's emails from this morning and reread them.

. . .

ISLA,

I NEED **you to call the post office again and get them to come out here to pick up the packages. Think that you can handle that?**

HUDSON

I ROLL my eyes and click on the next email he sent this morning.

ISLA,

I'M **sure that your to-do list is already overwhelming for you, but I need you to be a big girl and order me the following supplies.**

I SCAN the list of art supplies, my hands curling into fists the longer I read. My fingernails dig into the palms of my hands, and only then do I try to relax a bit. The freaking *audacity* of this man!

His little remark about my overwhelming to-do list is the cherry on top. I had the flu a couple of weeks ago and mentioned that I was flustered with getting caught up in one of my emails. It was a rookie mistake on my part. I know that now. Hudson has never shown empathy, or any other human emotion for that matter, so of course, he wasn't going to be understanding about me being sick or needing a day or two to catch up on things. The asshat has been bringing it up every chance since.

I take a sip of my tea and roll my shoulders back as I get ready to respond. As annoyed as I am, I can't deny the spark of adrenaline I get when I hit reply. A little smile tugs on the edges of my lips as I start to type.

It's time to get to work.

TWO

Hudson

I TAKE A CLOSER look at my latest sculpture, bending down to get a closer look at one of the edges. Running my fingers over the stone, I frown when I feel a bit of rough texture. I'll need to sand that down before taking the final shots and sending them to the client.

My computer dings, signaling a new email, and my heart takes off like a shot. It has to be Isla, my assistant. Despite my best efforts to calm my bear down, the bastard perks his ears up, ready for whatever sass the email contains.

I tried being annoyed with Isla for the longest time, but I can't deny that lately, the highlights of our day have been sparring with her. Isla is my first virtual assistant, lasting longer than a few weeks. I know I can be a little rough around the edges, but it's more than that. I want my art to be perfect. I have high expectations for myself, and I want my assistants to reach the same high standards. No one else has been able to keep up. No one until Isla.

Normally, I would only email my assistant a list of things once a week, but with Isla, I can't seem to stop myself from trying to provoke her. I'm the kid pulling the girl's pigtails because he likes her, but I doubt Isla would see it that way. She probably just thinks that I'm a jerk.

My bear snorts inside of me, lumbering to his feet and starting to pace. Even he is strangely interested in the assistant that we've never met in person before, and he usually doesn't seem to care about anyone. He's always been content to stay curled up inside of me, but for some reason, ever since Isla started to work for us, he's been restless. I have to take him out for a run almost every day now to burn off some of this energy.

I set my tools to the side, grabbing my rag and wiping off my hands before I pull my laptop closer so I can see the screen. We barely get service in this rundown town, which wasn't a problem at first. In fact, I liked it that way. It made it difficult to contact me and made for a good excuse when I didn't want to talk to other people. Being off the grid suited me just fine.

Until Isla. I can't explain the push and pull between us, but it's intoxicating. Now when the internet goes out, or the one cell tower out here goes down, I get antsy. If I don't have an open line of communication with Isla, my bear and I both start to go a little crazy.

It makes zero sense and, honestly, confuses the hell out of me. I've never had these... *feelings* for someone before, and clearly, I have no idea how to handle the intensity of it all.

Shoving all that aside, I tap on Isla's newest email, smirking as I start to read her words.

. . .

HUDSON,

NEED I remind you how lost you'd be without me? Imagine if you actually had to go out in public and purchase supplies yourself. The horror! As it is, I'm fully capable of the tasks you've given me.

I'M GRINNING from ear to ear by the time I finish her email. I don't know why I can't seem to stop antagonizing her. I should probably be careful not to push her too far. I can't have her quitting on me. Isla's words ring true - I would be lost without her.

She's the best assistant I've ever had, but it's more than that. I would miss her if she quit, and I know I'd never find someone else who interested and challenged me as much as she does.

I hit reply to email her back when my cell phone rings. For a second, I wonder if it's Isla calling to yell at me some more, and I practically dive to answer the call.

Instead of Isla's name on the screen, though, it's Alex, an old friend.

"Don't tell me that you're moving back to Twisted Oak," I say as I answer.

"God, no."

Alex just left this pack with his brothers, Max and Robin, and their adopted sister, Snow. They settled a little further west at the North Star pack a few weeks ago. I haven't talked to him much since, but he did text and send a picture of their new place.

My bear rumbles inside of me. He wants to leave this terrible pack, too. He's been pushing for it for years, but I've always held off. It's not like I hang out with the other pack members. Plus, it would be too hard to move my studio and all of my supplies. Then there's the fact that I'm not sure where I would move to. Would any other packs really be any better than here?

I have a million different excuses so I don't have to face the real reason I haven't left.

I deserve to live here with the terrible Twisted Oak pack filled with seedy characters and loners. I'm a monster, just like everyone else around here.

Monster. I've heard that word and been called that name more times than I can count growing up. I guess it was hard to see myself as anything else when I was surrounded by people who thought of me that way.

I grew up in a small town on the Washington/Oregon border. My parents left their pack and were raising me and my sisters there instead. I snuck out one night and headed to school. I had a spare key to the art studio and loved going there to work. Being in that studio that night probably saved my life.

When I went back home and snuck back into bed, I froze. I could smell it then. The scent of blood. To this day, when I close my eyes, I can still see the bodies of my family.

I shiver, trying to erase the image from my brain.

I called the police, but they never found out who killed them. I don't think they really tried, though. Everyone in that town was convinced that I was the one who had murdered them.

I was a big guy, even back then when I was just a

teenager, and no one believed me when I told them I was at the art studio at school. They couldn't picture a giant like me hunched over a pottery wheel or canvas.

I spent the next year at school all alone. No one would talk to me. I got dirty looks everywhere that I went. As soon as I had my diploma, I left that town and moved here. I knew that no one would bother me at the Twisted Oak pack. Even back then, it had a reputation of being a place for loners.

Somewhere over the years, that's changed to being a pack of loners *and* criminals, but still, I haven't tried to leave.

"Hello? Earth to Hudson. Am I interrupting a big project or something?"

"Huh? Oh, no, I'm good. Everything is good. What's up?" I ask, trying to pull myself from the memories and focus on my friend.

"Just calling to check on you. Have you left your studio in the last week?"

"Yes, Mom," I joke, and I can picture him rolling his eyes.

Alex, Max, and Robin are bear shifters like me. We bonded when I first moved to town, first over being bear shifters in a mostly wolf-dominated pack, but then it grew into a real friendship. It was weird but nice to finally have some people in my corner after a lifetime of being an outcast.

"What have you been up to?" he asks me.

"Just putting the final touches on a sculpture for a client. I should be done in the next day or two. How's the North Star pack?" I ask him.

"Really good. You should think about moving out here. It's nice not to have to constantly be worried about the people around you," he says, and my bear rumbles inside of me again. "Plus, I don't feel ashamed or like I have to make excuses whenever anyone asks which pack I belong to. I know you know what I'm talking about."

"Yeah," I grunt. " Well, maybe one day," I hedge, but we both know that probably won't happen.

"Why don't you come for a visit and see if you like it here?" Alex suggests.

"Do you have the room for me?"

"Yeah, Snow just moved in with her mate, so her room is free."

"Snow found her mate?" I ask in surprise.

Snow is human. She was taken in by the brothers and their parents when she was young. She was always nice to me, and I'm happy that she has a mate who will love and cherish her.

Yeah, good for her, but what about us? my bear growls bitterly. I ignore him like I do every time he brings up the fact that we haven't found our mate yet.

"Yeah," Alex sighs, and he sounds sad.

Alex, Max, and Robin have always been close to Snow. They were practically her shadow every time she left the house. I know the three of them are protective as hell, so I'm sure it's been a weird adjustment having her move out. I'm guessing they didn't make it easy for her mate to prove himself, but I'm glad everything seemed to work out in the end.

"Let me finish up this project, and then I'll see about a visit," I say.

I can't help but refresh my emails, desperate to see if Isla has said anything else. There are no new messages, and I sigh, closing my laptop and focusing on Alex.

"Okay, let me know. I'll talk to you later."

"Yeah, talk to you later," I say.

We hang up, and my stomach growls. I haven't eaten yet today, and I decide that now is as good a time as any to quit for the day.

Closing up my studio, I make sure that everything is locked up tight before I grab my laptop and head over to my little cabin.

My bear is pacing inside of me, more agitated than usual, and I try to calm him down.

I'll make us some food, and then we can go for a run, I promise him.

I don't want food and a run. I want my mate!

I sigh as I take out some bread and lunch meat. Of course, he's focused on this now after hearing about Snow.

A mate is the one thing that I can't give us. Who would love us? How would I find them? I can't imagine my fated one ever stepping foot onto the Twisted Oak land, and truthfully, anyone who finds a home here among the dredges of shifter society isn't someone I want to be mated to. Hypocritical? Maybe. But safe, nonetheless.

I eat, standing over the kitchen sink, staring out at the forest as the sun starts to set behind the trees. A sense of loneliness and sadness threatens to crush me; I try to take a deep breath. My eyes land on my laptop, and before I can stop myself, I start typing out another email to Isla, my only connection to normalcy.

This email is even snarkier than what I usually send her, and I hesitate to send it, but I can't seem to stop myself. I'm on a roll, and this is the only distraction that eases the pain in my chest. I hit send and take a deep breath, filling my lungs as a smile tugs at the edges of my lips.

I can't wait to see what she writes back to this one.

THREE

Isla

"WHYYY," I groan as I roll over in bed.

It isn't until I land on the floor that I realize I'm not in my bed.

"Umph," Hattie agrees, burrowing under the blankets.

I blink up at her through bleary eyes, wincing against the morning light. She's half on and half off of the couch, and I tug on the blankets until she slides down next to me.

"Just let me die," she rasps, and I shake my head.

Pain ricochets around my brain at the movement, and I squeeze my eyes tighter together.

"Don't move. It's terrible," I warn her. I swear I'm never touching alcohol again.

"Okay. I'll stay right here forever," she moans, tilting her head back before moaning again, louder this time.

My computer dings in the corner, and I hiss at it.

"Why would you leave the sound on," Hattie complains.

"I don't know. I have so many regrets," I groan.

Another email lands in my inbox, and we both wince at the loud ding.

"Please make it stop," Hattie begs. I use all my strength to push myself onto my hands and knees and shuffle across the old carpet to my desk. Has it always been so far from the couch? I swear our living grew by a quarter of a mile overnight.

"Ugh, whyyyy," I hiss as Hattie mumbles incoherently behind me. "It's so *bright*. How do I turn it down?"

"Throw it out the window," she suggests. I debate doing just that but decide against it.

"The sun's up. It's brighter outside than in here."

She sighs, burrowing under the blankets once more.

"I thought we were ride or die," I say sarcastically. My bestie bravely crawls out from under the blanket, though she keeps it wrapped around her face like a babushka.

"We could break it," she suggests. "Take a hammer to it and put it out of its misery."

"Too loud," I point out. She grunts.

"We could put it in the dishwasher."

I roll my eyes, regretting it instantly. My headache comes roaring to the surface. "No, I'll take one for the team."

I squint as I open the laptop again and hurry to find the volume button. I mute my computer and slam the lid closed.

"You're my hero," Hattie says, collapsing back onto the ground.

"What was in those drinks last night?" I whine pathetically.

"Tequila," she rasps, and I lean back against the wall.

"Never again."

"They were so good last night."

"Yeah, and that's the problem! They were so good, and we had too many. Now we're paying for it."

"I don't have work today. I'm going to bed."

"Brag."

"Good luck with your grumpy boss," she says, and I close my eyes before flipping her off. She giggles and then groans again as she gathers her bedspread and makes her way down the hall to her room.

I almost forgot about Hudson, which I suppose was the point. He was the reason Hattie and I went out last night. After his last email, I needed to blow off some steam. We ended up at our favorite Mexican restaurant right up the street, and she helped me brainstorm ideas.

I was ready to quit last night on the spot, but she reminded me that we have to pay for things like rent and food, so it looks like I'm still employed. We'll see if I still feel that way after reading whatever smartass emails he's surely sent already today.

Only one way to find out.

I heave my weary body upright and wobble my way into the bathroom. I need a shower to help me wake up. Then I'm going to drink an entire pot of coffee and try to find the will to stare at my computer screen and deal with clients for the next eight hours.

"Should have quit," I grumble as I lean against the wall outside the bathroom.

"Carbs, Isla. Think of the carbs. We can't buy them if you don't have a job!" Hattie yells from her room next door.

She's right. I need to be smart about this. It's just that sometimes when it comes to Hudson, I want to be really dumb. And petty. What can I say? He really brings out the best in me.

I stand under the hot water for way too long. By the

time I step out and wrap a towel around my body, however, I'm no closer to being awake. All I want to do is crawl back into bed, but I know that if I don't answer emails soon, then there's a pretty good chance that Hudson is going to call me. He's done it before, and I can't have that happening again.

There's just something about his voice. Rough, like gravel, with a deep baritone I swear I can feel all the way down to my toes. Every time I hear it, I break out into goosebumps and my stomach flips. I don't need my stomach doing any flipping today, *thankyouverymuch*. I don't want to tempt fate after a night of drinking.

That first phone call was brief. So brief, in fact, that I didn't have time to respond. Hudson just barked at me, ordering me to check my emails and do my job before he hung up. It had taken me ten minutes to snap out of my daze, and I was too confused and turned on to even be mad at him.

The bastard.

That was the first night I dreamt about him. The fantasies played like clockwork every night for a week after that before I was able to push him out of my head. I can't have him calling and starting the cycle all over again.

I throw on my comfiest clothes, an old pair of yoga pants and a stretched-out tank top before I head into the kitchen and straight for the coffee maker. It takes way too long to brew a pot, and I lean against the counter, tapping my toe impatiently as I watch the liquid drip, drip, drip into the pot.

When it's finally done, and I pour myself a cup, I almost burn my hand. Then I actually do burn my tongue and the roof of my mouth when I take a sip, but it's worth it when the caffeine hits my system.

I brace myself as I head over to my desk and settle in. I

check my emails first and sigh when I see that I have ten new ones to get through. Four of them are from Hudson, and I leave them for last. Naturally.

I respond to a few clients and write down the information for the gallery that wants to put on one of his shows to pass along to Hudson. Then I go back for more coffee before I click on his first email.

As soon as I read the opening line, I see red.

"I can't do this anymore," I spit.

"Carbs!" Hattie reminds me, and I grind my teeth, clicking out of the email and over to a job listing page that I bookmarked four months ago.

I apply to five new jobs before I click back on his email and keep reading.

ISLA,

TODAY IS A BUSY DAY, so I need you on top of your game, unlike most other days. Reply back when you get this, and I'll give you your first set of tasks.

Oh, where are my manners? *Please*, can you do your job today?

I CLICK on his next email and see that he is at least in a better mood for this one. Or, at least, he's not sarcastic.

ISLA,

.   .   .

THE MEYERS PIECE IS FINISHED. **I need you to arrange for shipping. I've attached the measurements for you.**

THE THIRD EMAIL is the measurements that he forgot to attach to the second email, and I roll my eyes, bracing myself as I click on his last message.

ISLA,

ARE YOU NOT WORKING TODAY? **What the hell am I paying you for? I know you like taking advantage of the relaxed work-from-home environment, but this behavior is unacceptable. I'm the moody artist, remember? I can't be the secretary, too.**

I'm used to subpar work and a terrible attitude from you, but at least you've never skipped out on work without so much as a fake flu excuse.

Do you even want this job?

"NO. I don't, actually. Screw the carbs," I snarl, and I swear that I hear Hattie start to weep. *Fake flu? Subpar work?* And which one of us has a terrible attitude? It's not just me, and he knows it.

I crack my knuckles, about to hit reply and tear into him, when a new email lands in my inbox. This one isn't from Hudson, luckily for him, but from one of the companies I applied to in a fit of rage last week.

I hurry to read it and grin when I see that they want to interview me. *This is it.* I'm free. I know I don't have the job yet, and the smart thing to do would be to wait until they make the offer to me, but I can't wait. Not with Hudson's angry, unfair words still fresh in my head.

I'm quitting. All of this rage and stress isn't good for me. I need to make a change.

My head and my heart are at war once again, but I'm not giving in to the inexplicable feelings I have for my boss anymore. Enough is enough. Today is the day, for real this time.

For someone who has threatened to quit nearly every day since being hired, I haven't put much thought into how I'd actually do it. Send him another email? Ghost him? Turn up to his house and lose it on him?

I like the last option the best, but I also know I have an ulterior motive there. I want to meet him face to face. Just once.

I bite my lip, debating. I could drive out to Twisted Oak and turn in my resignation. I could even be professional about it. That way, I get to satiate my curiosity about him a bit, and who knows, maybe if I can keep it pleasant and professional, he'll even give me a recommendation for this interview.

Ha. Yeah, freaking right.

"Hattie? I'm headed out for a bit! Let me know if you need anything!" I call as I slip on my shoes.

I'm out the door before I can think better of it or before she can ask me where I'm going and try to talk me out of it.

This is a good plan, I tell myself. *I'm going to quit and then be done with him for good.*

My pulse is racing as I slip behind the wheel of my old beater and crank the engine. It sputters, threatening to die but thankfully levels out.

This is it; I think as I punch in his address on my phone and hit the road.

It's a short drive to Twisted Oak, and I should be practicing what I'm going to say when I see him, but I can't seem to focus on that. Nerves and excitement swirl inside me, and as I hit the Twisted Oak town line, I tighten my grip on the steering wheel.

It feels like something big is about to happen. I just don't know what yet.

FOUR

Hudson

WHEN I HEAR the old car sputtering into my driveway, I assume that whoever's there is just turning around. Then when I see the pretty redhead climb out, I know they must be lost. *Perfect. Just what I need today.* Another woman to drive me insane.

My bear shifts inside me, raising his head in interest when we see her head toward the house. I should stop her, let her know I'm in the studio, and see what she wants, but I can't. I'm mesmerized by her curves, by the soft sway in her hips. *Who the hell is this woman?*

She seems a little nervous, her fingers twisting together over and over as she heads up to my front door. I've never seen someone so enchanting before. She can't be from town, and I can tell she's not a shifter. So what is she doing here?

Her lips are moving, and she looks like she's practicing a speech. It's kind of adorable, though my gut twists at the thought of her being nervous around me. I wish I could hear what she's saying, but she's talking too softly. Even with my advanced shifter hearing, I can't pick anything up.

Maybe she's here to sell something.

Buy whatever it is! my bear orders, and I roll my eyes at him.

Someone who looks like her is never going to get with someone who looks like us, I remind him, and he bares his teeth at me.

It's a reminder for me, too, and I grab a cloth, wiping the excess clay off my hands as I head out to see what she wants. The sooner I send this young woman on her way, the sooner I can deal with my missing assistant.

"Can I help you?" I call out. The woman jumps half a foot into the air, spinning around to face me. Her eyes are wide, obviously caught off guard, and as soon as I stare into their blue depths, my heart kicks against my ribs. Hard.

Something is happening to me, but I have no idea what. My bear is tense, on high alert the closer we get to the strange, enchanting woman. My chest grows tight as my heart continues to bash itself against my ribcage. *Am I about to pass out? What is going on?*

"Hudson," she says, her tone clipped. It's enough of a shock for me to get myself under control.

She knows me. It's not a question.

Her voice. It's so familiar. If I had met her before, I definitely would have remembered. No one could forget those big baby blues and sinful curves.

Which means that she can only be...

"Isla."

"Subpar work and a terrible attitude? *Fake flu?*"

I wince but try not to let her see how much I regret sending that.

I hadn't heard from her all morning, and she never responded last night. I was getting desperate for her attention, and it was a childish move, but I couldn't stop myself. Isla has me all kinds of messed up, but that's no excuse. My last email crossed a line, and I should never have hit send.

I can't come out and tell her that, of course. That's not how the game works.

"Yeah, I also asked if you were working today. I'm guessing it's a no to that question, too, since you're here and not at your computer."

It looks like she's about to breathe fire at me, and I find myself wanting to see that. It's been so long since anyone has seen me or really even talked to me. No one loses their cool around me. No one stands up to me. No one except Isla.

"You're the actual worst; do you know that?" Her face is bright red, and I won't lie; she looks absolutely radiant, surrounded by an aura of indignant rage and passion. I lean against my truck, watching her as she paces back and forth across my lawn.

She's ranting, throwing her arms up in the air to make her point, and I smile. She's beautiful. So full of life and beautiful, intense energy. I want to bottle it up so I can take a hit whenever I'm feeling uninspired.

Maybe that's what keeps drawing me back to Isla over and over. I enjoy our snarky emails and verbal sparring, but there's a pull between us. She's full of passion and purpose. Without knowing anything about her aside from our email exchanges, I can tell Isla has big dreams and enough motivation and enthusiasm to reach them when the time comes.

It's been so long since I had any of that. A part of me died along with my family all those years ago, and being around Isla... I feel like I'm finally waking up. Something about her makes me want to join the living again.

"You can't treat people like this!" she finishes, turning to glare at me. It was an impressive rant, even if I could only understand half of it with the way she was yelling.

My bear is watching her with interest. She's entertaining, sure, but it's more than that. It's like he's putting all the pieces of the puzzle together.

When the wind shifts, blowing her scent our way, we both figure out what we find so intoxicating about Isla at the same time.

"Mate," I whisper, straightening as my bear roars inside of my head. One big paw pushes against my chest, clawing and wanting to surge to the surface and claim her.

I can't do any of that right now, however. Biting her and demanding that she's mine would scare her off, and we can't have that.

My bear begrudgingly agrees, but he's no less on edge. *I've got this*, I tell him, though I'm not sure either of us believes me. What the hell do I know about relationships and mates? I've been a loner for so long, and I never thought I'd find my one true love. Then again, I didn't really find Isla. She came walking right up to my door.

"What?" Isla asks, pulling me from my spiraling thoughts. She has her hands on her perfectly rounded hips, and her blue eyes are narrowed in suspicion. God, she's gorgeous.

"Nothing," I tell her, needing to figure out a way to explain all of this to her without sending her for the hills.

"Really? I yelled at you for a solid five minutes and you have nothing to say back to me?"

It's hard to focus on what she's saying when my bear is

screaming in my head. I'm so focused on holding him back from breaking free that I can't concentrate on much else.

"You know what? I came here to quit respectfully but screw that and screw you."

Yes, let her screw us, my bear pleads, and I grit my teeth. *Not what she meant!*

"I quit, and I don't care if you write me a recommendation for my next job or not!" Isla finishes, her anger flaming around her.

Wait, quit? Oh, hell no.

"No," I snap, the panic truly setting in now.

"You don't get to boss me around, and you can't make me stay," she tosses over her shoulder as she starts to stomp back to her car.

"Isla, stop," I plead, but she keeps on walking.

I can't let her leave. Especially knowing how horrible that last email was to her. That can't be what she remembers me by. But how do I keep her? How do I make her listen?

I never thought I would find my mate. I never thought I deserved one. Plus, how do I explain that everyone thinks I killed my whole family? No one in the entire town believed me. Why would anyone?

Now that Isla is standing in front of me, though, I can't let her leave. My bear won't allow it. *This could be our chance,* he urges. *Our chance at another family. Our chance to be happy.* Dammit, he's right.

I'm moving before I have a plan on what to do. My only goal is to stop my mate from leaving. I need to try to explain this to her, and then I can make her see that we're meant to be.

"Wait," I say, my hand wrapping around hers.

A shock seems to pass through both of us, and she freezes, her eyes looking at our joined hands. I know she feels the pull, but it might not be strong enough. The mating connection is different for humans, or so I've been told. Still, she has to sense that I'm different. I'd never hurt her. All I want is for her happiness, and I know without a doubt I'm the only one who will love her and give her everything she could ever ask for.

Now I just need to figure out how to tell her that without sounding like a madman.

"I need you to stay," I say, trying to adopt a nicer tone. Her eyes snap up to meet mine, her brows furrowing in confusion. The questions in her blue depths give way to suspicion and finally back to anger.

"Yeah? For what? Give me one good reason why I should stay," she challenges me.

I take a deep breath, getting lost in her sweet scent.

She's human. I can't just tell her I'm a shifter and we're meant to be together. She would never buy that.

Still, I need to have that conversation with her soon...

"Because we're fated to be together," I tell her.

She stares at me blankly, not sure how to respond or if I'm just messing with her. I can see her studying me, trying to figure out how this could be a joke, but I'm dead serious.

"I mean it, Isla. We're meant to be together. And I can prove it."

She opens her mouth, then closes it again and frowns. Without thinking, I lift my free hand to her face, gently brushing away a few strands of her silky red hair. Jesus, her skin is so soft and creamy. I want to see my bite mark there. I want everyone to know she's mine.

"How?" Isla whispers, her eyes searching mine. I take a deep breath.

"It's a long story. Come inside, and I'll explain."

She definitely doesn't trust me, but she lets me tug on her hand and lead her inside. My bear is begging me to bite her and claim her, but I have a feeling that we won't be marking her for a while.

First, we have to make it through this conversation...

FIVE

Isla

THERE ARE a lot of words that I would use to describe Hudson. Talented, clever, abrasive, grumpy, a jerk. Now that I've seen him in person, I'd probably add handsome, tall, huge, maybe even hulking to that list. The guy could be an entire football team like he could rip trees out of the ground with one hand.

All that is shocking, but what's even more surprising is that before today, crazy wasn't one of those words I would use to describe him. But as I let him lead me into his house, I can't help but think he might have more than one screw loose.

Who just tells someone that they're meant to be together? That they're *fated* to be together?

What an odd choice of words.

My fingers tingle, and I know I should pull my hand from his, but it feels good to have his large, calloused fingers wrapped around mine. I feel safe, secure for the first time in years. Who knew that holding hands could do that?

His house is small. It's all just one room, and my eyes stray over to the giant bed shoved into the corner. I force myself to look away before my imagination can start to get wild, clearing my throat as I continue my inspection.

The place is rustic but neat. The whole cabin just seems bland. He's an artist. Where's the art? Where's the color? The walls and floor are made out of wood. Even the bed and counters seem to be made out of the same wood. It's not what I imagined his house would be like at all.

"I should get home," I say, my eyes straying to the door that I just walked in.

"Let me explain."

"You have five minutes," I tell him, trying to take back the upper hand here.

I need to keep my head around him. This could all be some trap, and then *bam!* I'm back to working for him and dealing with his grumpy ass for another year.

"We're fated to be together," he starts.

"So I've been told."

He sighs, scrubbing his hands down his face.

"I mean it."

"And you're just realizing this now? You've been bossing me around like an arrogant jerk for a year. That was you, what? Flirting?"

"Technically, I *am* your boss," he tells me, raising an eyebrow. "So bossing you around kind of comes with the job title." That was the wrong thing to say. I regret it immediately, but can't take it back.

"Actually, Hudson, if you would have been paying attention to my eloquent and impassioned speech outside, you'd know that you *aren't* my boss. Not anymore."

"I know you're not going to believe this," he says with a sigh, his broad shoulders sinking slightly.

"I don't," I interrupt him, and he growls.

"It's the truth, though."

"Right."

"Isla, I'm a shifter."

I stare at him blankly, trying to figure out what he means. "Like shifting from one weird mood to the next? I'm pretty sure there's medication for that nowadays."

"No," Hudson says exasperatedly. "I'm a bear shifter. All shifters have fated mates. You are mine. I knew as soon as I smelled you."

"You *smelled* me?"

"Yes," he nods, and I cross my arms over my chest.

So, he is crazy then...

"Shifters can smell their fated mate. It's this addictive sweet scent," he explains, and I can see him inhaling.

"Maybe I just smell good," I counter.

"No, that's not it."

"Gee, thanks," I deadpan, and he bites back a grin.

"I mean, it's not the same thing. My bear can smell it, too. He knew right away that it was more than perfume or body wash. You could feel it too. I know you could. When I touched you," he says, trailing off. I don't want to give him the satisfaction of being right, but my cheeks heat as I remember how it felt like a spark set off an explosion inside me when his hand touched mine.

I shift my weight from foot to foot, not wanting to admit he's right, but it's no use. He can read me too well.

"You're meant to be our mate."

"And if I don't believe you and don't want to be your mate?"

"Then I'll prove it to you," he says, his jaw tight with determination.

"Why would I want to be with you? You've been a jerk to me for as long as I've known you."

"I can change."

"Can I trust that, though? What happens if you go back to being mean and grumpy?"

"I'll probably always be grumpy," he admits, and I appreciate that he can be honest about that. "I can be what you want, what you need. Fate wouldn't have put us together otherwise. What are you looking for in a mate?"

"Well, for starters, someone who doesn't call me mate like some kind of caveman."

"Noted. Lover."

"Oh, god, no. Try girlfriend."

"But you're so much more to me than that," he says dismissively.

It's like the suggestion that I be his girlfriend has insulted him.

"You're my everything. Girlfriend doesn't encompass that. It's insufficient in every way."

"We can argue that later. You have two more minutes to explain whatever you need, and then I'm leaving."

"No, you're not," he says easily. I growl at him.

He blinks, a smile spreading on his face, and my stomach turns over. Seeing him smile transforms his whole face, his whole presence.

"Hudson," I bark, and he blinks again.

"Sorry, that was cute."

I do my best to ignore my body's reaction to hearing him call me cute and focus on the conversation.

"Do you want to meet my bear?"

"Uh, yeah," I say. "Sure. Turn into a bear."

Out of everything he's said, this is the part that makes me think he's way off his rocker. He'll show me some stuffed animal or something, and then I'll know for sure that I should call some institution and head home.

He reaches for his shirt, tugging it over his head, and my brain shortcircuits as I stare at his sculpted chest and arms.

"Holy muscles, batman," I mumble, but he ignores me.

He reaches for his pants, and I hold my hand out, stopping him before he can push the sweatpants down his legs.

"Sorry, what's happening here?" I blurt, and he frowns.

"I'm taking off my clothes," he explains slowly like *I'm* the crazy one.

"Got that, asshole. What I meant was *WHY?*"

"So I don't rip them."

"Are you going to hulk out or something? I'm not sure that this cabin is big enough for that."

"Smartass," he mumbles, shoving his pants and boxers down his legs.

He kicks his shoes and clothes to the side as I pretend to find his kitchen sink fascinating.

"Are you watching?" he asks, and I shake my head.

"Nope. If I wanted to see some guy's dick, then there's porn, or I could pick some guy up at a bar or—"

"The only cock you're looking at from now on is mine. Is that clear?" Hearing him take that bossy tone has me pressing my thighs together for some messed up reason. What is this throbbing ache deep in my core?

Shoving that aside, I try to remain focused and in control. "We'll see," I reply.

I can't seem to help myself. I love riling him up. I want to see what he'll do if I push him just a little bit more...

"Isla," he says in a gravelly tone, and I blink, staring up at the ceiling.

"I mean, a girl has needs," I tell him with a shrug. "What if your cock can't satisfy those needs?" I ask innocently, and he growls.

"Trust me. I can. Though, it doesn't seem like I even need my cock to satisfy you. I can smell your arousal already, and I haven't even touched you yet," he says smugly.

I gasp, my eyes flying to his, and he's smirking at me.

"I was thinking about some other guy," I lie, and he growls, his eyes flashing at me in warning.

"You have thirty seconds," I remind him, taking a step backward toward the door.

"Watch," he orders, and I nod.

It's a good thing that I am watching, or I never would have believed it.

It happens so fast. One second, I'm arguing with Hudson, and the next, there's a bear standing where he just was.

"Fuck!" I scream, leaping up onto his couch.

The bear blinks at me, and I stare back in shock. He shifts again, and I'm still gawking at Hudson as he tugs his pants back on.

"Why are you on the couch?" He asks me, and I stare at him in shock.

"To get away from the freaking bear!"

"Right. Well, first, I need you to understand that if it was a wild bear, jumping up onto furniture or anything else wouldn't save you."

"You're the actual worst," I spit out at him, and he shakes his head.

"You would never make it here in Twisted Oak," he says more to himself than to me.

"And why's that?"

"Too many shifters and other animals around."

"There's more shifters here?" I ask as I climb down from the couch.

"More like monsters," he mumbles, and I frown.

"What does that mean?"

"The people who live here in the pack, they're not... well, we're not good," he explains, and a piece of my heart breaks when I realize that he includes himself in that.

Sure, Hudson can be a pain in my ass. He can be grumpy, cold, and frustrating, but I would never call him a monster.

Hudson clears his throat, obviously uncomfortable with me feeling pity for him.

"The full moon is tomorrow. You can stay until then. I'll bite you, and we'll be mated then."

"I'm a goldfish from Mars," I reply, and he stares at me like I'm crazy.

"What?"

"Oh, I thought we were just saying crazy things that mean nothing to no one."

He rolls his eyes, but I can see him fighting back a smile.

"Shifters mate on the full moon. The mating heat is going to hit both of us pretty hard tomorrow. Shifters bite their fated mates and mark them. It helps to bond us together," he explains, and I sigh.

"I'm going to need you to explain all of this shifter stuff better."

"I will. Let me make up the bed for you first for whenever you're tired."

My phone rings, and I pull it out to see that Hattie is calling me.

"I should get this."

He nods, and I step outside.

"Don't leave," he says, following after me.

I nod, but I can see the worry in his eyes.

"I won't. I promise," I tell him, and he relaxes and heads inside.

"Hey," I answer, and she yawns.

"Where are you? Did you quit?"

"Kind of…"

"How do you kind of quit?"

"It's complicated," I sigh, and she chuckles.

"When are you coming home? I just got called in to work. I can pick up a shift tonight, so I'm about to head out."

"I actually think I'm going to end up staying here tonight," I admit slowly.

There's a beat of silence, and I close my eyes, knowing what's about to come.

"Why? Oh my gosh! Did you two finally get past the sexual tension now that you're together? Are you doing him right now?"

"Yep," I deadpan, and she laughs.

"I knew you liked him! All that bickering and arguing was just so you both could try to ignore the sexual tension between you two!"

"What sexual tension? I just met the guy today!"

"You don't need to meet someone to love them. You can fall in love through letters," she says, and there's a wistful tone to her words that makes me wonder if she knows firsthand.

"I don't like him," I try to protest, and she laughs again. "I don't! It's just… it's complicated."

"Uh-huh," she says with a laugh.

I don't like keeping things from Hattie, but how am I supposed to explain any of this to her? She'll think I'm crazy. I'd think that I was crazy.

"Well, have fun figuring out if you're going to jump his bones or quit. I'll talk to you later."

"Hilarious. See you later," I say, and she laughs as she hangs up.

I turn back to the house, staring at the front door, and realize then that she's right. I need to figure out what the hell I'm doing.

Do I believe that we're meant to be? No, but I can't deny that there's something happening between us.

I just want to see where it leads. Then I'll leave.

I promise.

SIX

Hudson

I PACE back and forth in my small living room while Isla finishes up her call out on the porch. Running my hands through my hair, I tug at the strands as if that will somehow rattle an idea loose in my brain. No such luck, however.

Grabbing a fresh set of sheets from the closet, I begin changing the sheets and preparing Isla's bed. The whole time, I'm trying to think of what I'm going to say. How am I going to make Isla see that we're perfect for each other when I've spent the last year doing my best to annoy her? From her rant earlier, I've gathered that she thinks I've done much more than just annoy her. I went too far. She's not just angry; she's... hurt.

My bear whimpers inside my chest, and I deflate when I realize the damage I've done. Isla is my fated mate, my one true love, the most precious, important person in the universe to me. I didn't know it at the time, but that's no excuse.

If it wasn't already obvious, let me just say that I have zero experience with dating or the opposite sex. I have no idea how to apologize, let alone woo someone.

I can't let her leave without trying, though.

I wish my parents were still here to talk to them about this.

A familiar ache forms in my chest, and I rub at it absentmindedly. My bear rumbles, and I can feel his sadness too.

I know, buddy. I miss them too.

The door opens, and I straighten as Isla comes back inside. I'm just finishing up placing the last blanket on top, and her eyes go to the bed.

"I only have the one bed, so I'll take the couch," I tell her.

We both glance over to the small sofa, and I wince as I imagine trying to get any sleep on that thing. My bear starts to pace, and I sigh. The truth is that I would sleep on top of the stove if that made Isla comfortable enough to stay here with me and give this a chance.

"Right," she says as I toss a pillow onto the bed.

Turning to Isla, I get momentarily caught up in her crystal blue eyes. There's such depth hidden beneath layers of sass and beauty. I need to know everything about her, and I need to know right now.

"Tell me about yourself," I ask, though it comes out hard and more like an order.

"What do you want to know?"

"Everything."

"Right. Well, um, I'm between jobs right now," she starts, making me grin. God, I love this woman.

"Yeah? I'm actually looking to hire myself right now. Tell me about your last job."

"Well, it was actually a pretty cool gig. The only downside was my boss."

"Overbearing?"

"Oh, yeah. He could be a real bear," she says with a smirk.

A strange sensation takes over me, one I can't say I've felt since... well, since before my family was taken from me. Before I can stop it, a hearty laugh escapes my mouth. Isla peers up at me, her eyes sparkling with mischief and more than a little lust. My bear jumps onto his hind legs, but I calm him down. *Not yet, but soon.*

Hopefully.

"What else?" I ask.

"Well, he was grumpy and could be cold."

"Sounds like you're lucky to have gotten away," I say, my stomach sinking.

Did I already lose her? Did I push her away before she was ever even mine?

"Well, we'll see."

Hope sparks to life inside me, and my bear starts to pace back and forth.

Woo her! Make her fall for us, and then she'll never want to leave.

I freeze at that thought. She has to leave, though. A princess like my Isla can't stay here and live amongst the monsters. Her light and life are too precious to be snuffed out by these cruel creatures. She'd never be happy in such a small town, and I would always be worried about her.

My bear growls inside of me. He's not at all happy about the thought that our mate wouldn't always be with us.

It would be what's better for her, though, I remind him, and he snarls at me.

We can protect her.

Like we did our family?

He whines, and I know that was a low blow.

We can't always be with her, I try again, and he rumbles, resuming his pacing. *She'll be close by. We can go visit her anytime.*

He's not thrilled with my compromise, but at least I don't have to worry about him trying to break free and claim her anymore.

Maybe if I had been part of a pack when I was younger, I would miss it more now. Maybe my parents and sister would never have been killed, and I wouldn't have been labeled a monster. Maybe then I could have a happily ever after ending, but it's not in the cards for me.

"I live with my best friend, Hattie. We've been friends forever and moved out together as soon as we turned eighteen and graduated."

"Do you have any siblings?" I ask her, and she shakes her head.

"No, we were both only children. She was the closest that I had to a sibling."

"I'm glad that you had someone so close to you."

"Me too. Hattie is the best," she says with a wide smile.

"What about your parents?" I ask her, and she hesitates.

"They're... fine."

I raise my eyebrows at her vague answer, and she shrugs.

"Honestly, I think they forgot they had a daughter most of the time. Quite literally, actually. I can't count the number of times they were supposed to pick me up from school or piano practice, only to wait outside for hours until someone took pity on me and gave me a ride."

"Isla," I murmur. I can't imagine anyone ignoring this

lively, vivacious woman. How could they not see how special she is?

"It's fine," she says with a shrug. "Hattie's parents were like that, too. They weren't very supportive. We left as soon as we could and headed to San Francisco, though we probably should have done some more prep work. When we ran out of money, Hattie and I knew we couldn't go back home. Neither one of us had heard from our parents since we left. Still haven't. Anyway, going home wasn't an option, so we moved to a small town where we would be able to pay rent."

We stand in silence, letting her confession sit between us. I'm not sure what to say, what words could possibly suffice for her basically being abandoned by her parents. It's such a different life from my own, but I know that if she gave me a chance, neither of us would have to be lonely anymore.

"I'm so sorry," I murmur, taking a step closer to my beautiful mate.

"I'm fine," she says once more. There's that word again. *Fine.* It's not fine, though. She should never feel less than or like she's an afterthought. I'll prove to her she's the first and only thing on my mind; all she has to do is give me a chance.

Isla chews on her bottom lip, looking around the cabin, and I wonder if she likes it here.

"Why don't you show me around town?" Isla suggests, and I startle.

"God, no!"

She blinks, caught off guard by my harsh reaction.

"Um, okay?"

"I... it's not safe here," I rush to explain. "I can show you my studio, though," I offer, trying to make her happy.

"Sure, show me where the magic happens."

I raise an eyebrow, pointing to the neatly made bed, and she rolls her eyes.

"Right." I don't miss the blush creeping up her cheeks or the hint of arousal I can smell. My mate is feeling the pull of the mating moon, that's for sure. I just hope I can earn her trust and her heart as well.

Isla heads outside, and I follow after her, breathing in her sweet scent. My bear and I want to roll around in it. We want her scent covering us and all of our things.

I let her into the small art studio, instantly regretting it. The scent of clay and turpentine is strong here, overpowering my mate's delicious scent. I'd like to grab and drag her back outside, but she's already walking around the small space.

"What are you working on now?" she asks me as she circles the canvas I put up just before she arrived.

"I was thinking about painting something, actually. I need a break from sculptures for a minute. I finished that piece this morning, though," I say, nodding to the sculpture half wrapped in protective paper.

"Ah, the one you wanted me to arrange shipping for," she remembers.

I nod as she walks closer and takes it in. The sculpture is of a couple embracing. Their limbs are wrapped around each other so completely that you don't know where one ends and the other begins. It's one of my best works to date, and I love how it turned out.

"It's beautiful," Isla says quietly. The sincerity and awe in her voice nearly bring me to my knees. I never knew why I dove into art or where my inspiration came from, but now I understand. It was all for Isla. She's my reason for creating. My bear and I beam with pride.

"Thank you."

"So, you paint too, then?" she asks, turning back to me.

It takes me a few seconds to respond. I'm too caught up in her soft curves, round, slightly blushed cheeks, button nose, and full, pouty lips.

Clearing my throat, I finally find my words. "I dabble. Usually, I'll pick it up when I need a change of pace. I'm not as good with a brush as I am with clay, though."

"How about with a frying pan?" Isla asks, and I blink.

"Are you hungry?"

"Starving. I haven't eaten yet today," she admits.

"Can't have that. Let's go see what I have in the fridge."

I lead the way back inside and let Isla see what I have in the fridge and pantry. She decides on grilled cheese and soup, and I'm just grateful that it's something I can make.

We can show her that we can take care of her, my bear agrees, and I get to work.

I'm hyper-aware of where Isla is in the cabin. Every cell in my body craves her. I want to fill my lungs with her scent as I bury myself inside of her; I want to sink my teeth into her creamy skin and feel her shudder out an orgasm all around me as I bring her more pleasure than she's ever experienced.

First, I need to make her dinner.

SEVEN

Isla

I DIDN'T SLEEP for a single second last night.

I'm trying to convince myself it's just because I've never spent the night with a man, or perhaps that I'm in a new, strange environment. But deep down, I know the real reason. It's that mating moon Hudson was telling me about. Something about fated mates craving each other, a nearly unbearable need to be together.

Rolling onto my back on the soft mattress, I stare up at the wooden ceiling, much like I did for hours on end last night. I counted the wooden beams while listening to every sound that Hudson made. Every time he shifted on the couch. Every breath and sigh. I was awake for all of it.

I don't think Hudson got too much sleep, either. His breathing never really evened out, and he seemed as sexually frustrated as I was. As much as I hate to admit it, the mating heat is even stronger this morning. It feels like it grows stronger with every passing second.

When I first showed up here and heard his ridiculous exclamation that I was his mate, I was positive I wouldn't agree to it. Then he turned into a freaking bear in front of me, and my body couldn't seem to function without his hands on me. Strange, since Hudson has barely touched me at all.

Now, it's all I can think about.

If I'm feeling like this, doesn't that mean something? Maybe we really are meant to be. Maybe Hattie was right, and the reason I stuck it out with this job for so long was because I could sense there was something else between us.

Does some part of me want Hudson? Yes, but is that a good idea? We haven't exactly gotten along since we met. Is that what I want in a partner? Is that what's going to make me happy? Am I just overthinking things?

I need to see how things go today. There's still time for me to leave and head back to our apartment before the full moon tonight if things don't go well.

I sit up in bed, and Hudson instantly does the same, like he was waiting for me to wake up before he moved.

"Um, good morning," I say, my voice coming out raspy and sleepy.

"Morning. How did you sleep?" he asks, but I get the sense that he already knows the answer to that.

"Good," I lie. "Thanks for letting me sleep in your bed."

"Anytime," he says with a groan as he climbs off the couch.

I watch as he rolls his shoulders back and shuffles toward the kitchen to start the coffee maker.

"Are you hungry?" he asks as I climb out of the bed.

"Not yet. I think I need a shower to wake up first."

"Help yourself," he says, nodding toward the bathroom.

His eyes seem to heat and almost glow as I move closer

to the bathroom door, and I wonder if he's imagining me in the shower, naked, water running in rivulets down my body. My heart starts to race as I picture it, and for one second, we stare at each other, tension, a connection growing stronger between us.

I blink first, turning without a word and hurrying into the privacy of the bathroom. I turn the shower on, cranking the water as hot as it will go, then strip out of my borrowed clothes. Hudson had insisted that I use some of his clothes to sleep in. I think it added an extra layer of intimacy, turning me on even more as I was surrounded by his scent all night.

I leave the clothes on the sink and step under the spray, sighing as the hot water relaxes the tension from my muscles. As I smooth the soap over my extra-sensitive skin, I can't help but picture Hudson in here with me, his rough hands gliding down my body, squeezing my breasts while I moan and melt against him.

Sliding my own hand down my body, I dip two fingers into my throbbing core, nearly doubling over at my own touch. Everything is swollen and sensitive, begging for more. But not by my own hand. My body wants Hudson.

Shaking my head of those thoughts, I hurry up, rinsing off so I can get back out to Hudson. Whether I decide to be his mate or not, something in me is desperate to be near him. At least for now. I can see where things go, and maybe... I don't even know. Am I crazy for seriously considering this entire situation? Being mated to my jerk of a boss?

I step out of the shower and debate walking out in a towel to grab my clothes from last night or putting Hudson's clothes back on. I think some part of me wants to tease him, to see what he'll do, so I wrap the fluffy blue towel around my body and walk out of the bathroom in a cloud of steam.

"Fuck me," Hudson groans quietly as I walk over to the bedside table and grab my clothes.

"What was that?" I ask him with a smile, and he blinks.

"How about I make you some breakfast?" he says, side-stepping my question.

"Sure."

I head back into the bathroom and get dressed. By the time I come out, the small cabin smells like bacon.

"Where do you go grocery shopping? I don't think I saw a market or anything on my drive in."

"There's a small shop a few miles south of here. I usually go there."

"Maybe we should go today. There wasn't much left in the fridge or pantry," I point out.

"I can go," he says quickly, and I frown.

He really didn't want me going into town or around the area yesterday either, and I'm starting to grow suspicious.

"Is there, like, someone in town you don't want to run into or something?" I ask. An ache bubbles up in my chest, and I wonder if he's... embarrassed of me? Because I'm a human instead of a shifter? Ouch. That hurts more than it should.

Hudson blinks at me a few times before answering. "Yeah, everyone."

"What? You don't want to see anyone? Why do you live here if you hate everyone?"

"I don't... well, it's..." he lets out a long breath that speaks louder than words. It's filled with a weariness that breaks my heart. "The people, the shifters who are part of this pack, are all loners, like me. But they aren't just anti-social. A lot, most even, are criminals and just... they're not good people. I don't want you around them. If anything ever happened to you..."

He shakes his head as if the thought of me getting hurt pains him. I won't lie; the fact that he wants to protect me is sweet, which isn't something I ever thought I'd say about Hudson. He wants me to feel safe and at ease here, which is more than most people in my life.

That also means that he sees himself as a loner and a bad person, too. Why else would he continue to live here? He called them monsters last night. Is that really how he sees himself? How is that possible?

Another piece of my heart breaks for him, and suddenly, I want to know everything I can about my grumpy mate. He's much more complicated than I originally gave him credit for, and it's now my new priority to peel back the layers of his past and make him see what I see.

"Tell me about yourself," I say as I take a seat at the kitchen table and watch him cook us breakfast.

"There's not much to tell."

"Well, I don't believe that for a second."

He grimaces, and I settle in, my curiosity piqued.

"I was born into a tiny pack in Oregon, but my parents left and took my sister and me to Poley, Washington, when I was really young. I grew up there."

"I've never heard of that city."

"I'm not surprised," he says with a chuckle. "It's tiny. The population is only about two hundred, and it's half buried in the forest. It was pretty remote."

"Are your parents and sister still living there?" I ask him.

The hint of a smile on his lips fades away, and he looks away from me sharply.

Hudson flips the bacon in the pan and clears his throat. I almost tell him he doesn't have to answer, but he clears his throat again and begins to speak.

"My parents and sister were killed several years ago," he says quietly. My chest caves in at his confession, each word sinking like a lead bullet. "Home invasion," he adds. "Middle of the night. I wasn't... I didn't... I couldn't protect them."

"Hudson... I'm so sorry," I murmur. A million thoughts race through my head, but one thing he said sticks out more than the rest. This giant Greek god of a man who literally turns into a badass bear whenever he wants is guilt-ridden for not saving his family.

I feel so stupid. I had googled Hudson when I first started working for him, but there was barely any information about him aside from his artwork. Now that he mentions it, though, I remember a short article about him being arrested for their murders. I hadn't believed it and had assumed that it was about a different Hudson. What the hell?

"The entire town assumed I was the one who did it," he tells me, and I feel tears stinging the back of my eyes. "I wasn't home when it happened," he chokes out. "Snuck out to the high school art studio to work on a project, and when I came home..."

"You found your family..." I can't even finish the thought. How awful, how traumatizing to have your family not only taken from you but to find their bodies? And then to have no time to grieve before everyone points fingers at you.

I'm out of my seat before I can think better of it. Hudson looks as surprised as I do, and as he turns to face me, I wrap my arms around his torso and cling to the beastly, broken, beautiful man who has stolen my heart.

EIGHT

Hudson

I'M SURROUNDED by my mate's scent, her arms wrapping around me as she presses her curvy body against the hard slats of my muscles. I can't remember the last time someone hugged me or, hell, gave me a handshake.

I didn't realize how starved for physical contact I was, and to now have my mate in my arms... it's almost too much. My bear claws at my throat, wanting to mark her, but I will him back inside. This moment isn't about that. It's raw and pure and something I've never experienced before.

I feel... complete. In every conceivable way. My mate fits perfectly right here in my embrace, and I know deep down in my bones we belong together. I'm hers as much as she's mine. I just hope she doesn't leave me when she realizes I got the better end of the deal when it comes to fated mates.

Isla buries her face into my chest, and I quickly turn off

the stove, realizing this is more important than breakfast. For now.

I hold my precious girl close, wrapping one arm around the small of her back while my other hand combs through her red locks. Tilting my head down, I nuzzle into the top of her head, breathing her in and letting everything about my mate consume me.

We don't say anything for long moments; we just let this feeling, this contact be enough. Isla has my heart in her hands. She could crush it in an instant, but instead, she's healing me in ways I didn't know I was broken. I don't deserve her, but I'll spend the rest of my life keeping her happy and safe.

"There's no way you did it," Isla whispers. Something loosens from my chest, a weight I didn't know I was carrying. I know I didn't do it, but hearing someone else say it out loud is freeing, in a way. "I don't believe it for a second."

I peel her off my chest, cupping her cheek and angling her head so we're eye-to-eye. Searching her blue depths, I see nothing but genuine concern and heartbreak. There's no judgment or fear, which is a relief. I wasn't sure how Isla would handle the information about my family, but of course, she took it in stride. She's my perfect mate.

"Thank you," I murmur. "Thank you for believing me. No one's ever…" I trail off, dropping my hand and looking away from her intense gaze. My mate surprises me by cupping my face, much like I did hers. She caresses the stubble on my cheek, and I close my eyes, leaning into her touch.

"You're not a monster," Isla says softly. "You're not a criminal or a bad person. You did nothing wrong. You know that, right?"

I blink a few times, clearing my eyes of what surely can't

be tears. I haven't cried, not even one tear, since that night all those years ago. But this woman, this incredible, sassy, sweet, kind, and understanding woman, is bringing out things in me I didn't know I was capable of. I hope she sees it, too. That it's more than the mating moon and the physical pull, it's our hearts. They're bound together forever.

"It's hard to believe that when I've been told the opposite for so long. I know I didn't kill my family directly, but I still failed them. Where was I when they needed me the most? Out doing my own selfish thing. If I was there, I would have..."

"Would have what?" Isla counters. "There's nothing you could have done. Hudson, you would have been killed right along with your family, and then I would have never had the chance to know you."

My eyes widen at her words as hope blooms in my chest.

"God, that sounds awful of me," she sputters. "I'm so sorry. I didn't mean any disrespect to your family or to dismiss you; I just... what if we never met? I can't explain why it hurts so much to think that." She blinks up at me with watery eyes, and I see that she's just as devoted to me as I am to her. She feels my pain like I feel hers. I never thought I would be whole or understood, but right here, with my mate, all is right in my world. I'll do anything to keep her as mine.

"Isla," I whisper, resting my forehead on hers as my hands find her hips. "There's nothing to apologize for. The fact that you care, that you took my side, that you even want to know me after some of the things I've said to you means more than I could ever express."

We stay frozen in time and space, our foreheads touching, our lips mere inches apart, our breaths mingling in the silence of the morning. I can hear my mate's heart beating out a rapid rhythm, her breathing growing shallow as she shifts forward slightly, pressing herself against me.

She tilts her head up as I tilt mine down, our lips meeting in the middle for our first kiss. I'm instantly addicted to her taste, her soft, pliant mouth as she opens up for me and lets me slide my tongue inside. Isla moans so sweetly, so urgently, as I lick the roof of her mouth before tangling my tongue with hers.

My hands slip from her hips to her round, full ass, and I squeeze her firm cheeks while helping her grind against me. Everything she does is explosive, from the way her fingers crawl up my chest and tangle in my hair to her soft, needy whimpers as I give her everything we both want.

Walking us back a bit, I lean Isla against the counter, crowding her space and inhaling her sweet scent as her lips find mine once more. I grip her thigh, lifting it up and hooking her leg around my hip, opening her up even more.

Isla moans into my mouth as I grind my hard as fuck cock into her soft, warm center. I know the exact moment I rub against her most sensitive spot. Her entire body spasms, her breath catches in her throat, and the smell of her arousal grows impossibly stronger.

I want to see it. I want to taste it. I want her essence on my tongue before I slide nine inches deep in that perfect little pussy. As if reading my mind, Isla digs her fingernails into my shoulders, pulling me closer, needing me as much as I need her.

We finally break apart, gasping for breath as our heartbeats slow down and sync up.

"Holy shit," she says, still struggling to get enough air. I grin, nodding in agreement. "Can we do that again?"

NINE

Isla

HUDSON GROWLS, and the next thing I know, he's sweeping me up into his arms and carrying me toward his bedroom, bridal style. I giggle at his eagerness and then gasp when he tosses me down on his bed, falling on top of me and kissing me breathless once again.

"You drive me crazy, mate," he growls, burying his face into the side of my neck and breathing me in. "You smell so damn good," he mumbles. "Bet you taste even better."

With that, he rips my shirt open, growling when he sees I have no bra on before leaning down and sucking on my nipples. Hudson grunts around a mouthful of my breast, the vibrations rocking me to my core. I can't explain the sudden need to feel his teeth on my skin, the sting of his bite, and the release I know will follow.

"Need you naked, Isla. Need to see all of you. Every single inch." He sounds like he's in pain. Hudson is not the kind of man who would beg for anything, but I can hear the desperate plea in his voice. Knowing he wants me that much makes me feel unbelievably sexy and powerful.

I push him off me, giving him what I hope is a sexy, teasing smile. It must work because his eyes turn dark and stormy the moment he realizes this is really going to happen, that I want him as much as he wants me.

I move to take off the rest of my clothes, but Hudson stops me.

"That's my job, beautiful mate." He continues to undress me slowly, pulling down my pants and scattering sweet kisses along my skin as he goes. I've never felt more vulnerable in my life and yet completely safe and seen.

When I'm fully naked before him, Hudson stands back and looks me over from head to toe. If I found myself in this scenario a week ago, I would try to cover myself up and hide. The idea of anyone else seeing me so exposed is almost inconceivable.

But there's no doubt that Hudson likes what he sees. His jaw tenses, his nostrils flare, and his hands clench into fists at his sides. The already impressive bulge in his pants swells even bigger, making me lick my lips.

"Jesus Christ, you're even better than I imagined. Get on the bed, Isla, and spread your legs. Let me see your pretty pussy."

I don't hesitate to follow his command. Once I'm spread out for him on the bed, he stands in front of me and stares right between my legs. Again, I should be shy or embarrassed, but the way he's looking at me banishes every single thought except that one word. *More.*

He wipes a hand down his face and shakes his head as if pulling himself out of a trance. Slowly, Hudson peels his shirt off, revealing his hard, delicious muscles. I can't wait to feel them pressed up against my chest while he's sliding in and out of me.

My dirty thoughts have more wetness leaking out of me. I feel it drip down my slit and tickle my back entrance, making me shiver. Hudson practically snarls, his eyes locked onto my core. He makes quick work of the rest of his clothes and strokes his massive cock.

"I don't even know where to begin," he says more to himself than to me.

His confession makes me bold. I slide my hand down my torso and dip my fingers into my pussy, rubbing my clit and then spreading myself open for him. "How about right here?"

"Fuck," he groans, falling to his knees and dragging my ass to the edge of the bed. He bats my hand away and buries his face between my thighs, sucking on my folds and making me cry out.

My hips shake as my entire pelvis bucks forward, making Hudson growl while he continues to drag his tongue over my most sensitive skin. Every muscle pulls tight against my skin, both wanting more and needing relief from the sweet torture of my mate's demanding licks.

I come viciously, my body jerking forward as pleasure trickles through every vein. Hudson grunts and laps up my release. "Again," he says into my throbbing cunt, licking me up and down, over and over, keeping me right on the edge and then throwing me over into another orgasm.

He places sloppy, opened-mouthed kisses up my stomach and between my breasts while I float back down to earth. When he kisses me, I taste myself on him and moan, deepening our kiss until Hudson pulls back and gasps for air.

"Ready, mate?" he asks, rubbing his hard cock up and down my slit.

"Yes," I breathe out, nodding my head. "Please make me yours. I want to be your mate."

He stops breathing for a second and then rests his forehead on mine. "Love hearing you say that," Hudson breathes out. He takes a second to compose himself, then looks at me with such reverence I almost feel like crying. "Do you trust me?"

"With all my heart," I don't hesitate to answer.

"That's what I like to hear, sweet girl. I promise I'll make it so good for you." He presses his dick inside me, just a little bit, stretching me wide open. "Relax, Isla. Let me in," he murmurs, burying his face into the side of my neck as he thrusts all the way inside.

A second later, Hudson's teeth sink into my neck, the spark of pain heightening the liquid bliss coursing through my body. I clench myself around him, my pussy twitching with each new wave of pleasure.

"Hudson, please," I whimper, grinding myself against him uncontrollably.

He grunts, then drags his tongue over my mark, the sensation rolling through every cell of my body as my mate pulls his massive length out and slides back inside.

"Yes!" I gasp. "Please, I need you to move."

Instead of answering, Hudson hisses out a breath and angles his hips before backing off and slowly entering me again. I feel his thick cock slide against the walls of my pussy in shallow, controlled thrusts. But that's not what I want.

"More, mate, I need more."

Hudson pulls almost all the way out and stares between

us, where the evidence of my virginity is smeared on his cock. We both groan at the sight.

I cry out when he slams home in one hard thrust, rocking me to my very core. One hand glides down my body, cupping my breast, then kneading the soft flesh of my hips. I've always been self-conscious of my curves, but they fit perfectly in Hudson's hands as he caresses and worships every inch of me.

Hudson continues his exploration of my body, sliding his hand up and down my outer thigh. He grips me behind my knee, opening me up more for him and pressing my leg up against my chest.

"Oh my God, yes, yes, yes!" I moan. At this angle, he's hitting that spot again, the one that sparks every single nerve ending I have and makes me shake uncontrollably.

"There it is. So. Fucking. Hot," he groans in between rough strokes.

My pussy gushes for him, our bodies making wet, sticky sounds as we grind against each other and chase after our pleasure. Hudson buries his face into the side of my neck and grunts each time he hits home, his teeth finding the divots of my mark and biting down with excruciating bliss.

I feel my muscles tense and pull tight against my skin as he pounds into me over and over, splitting me open and demanding my orgasm. My entire body throbs, not understanding what's about to happen but wanting it anyway.

"I feel you, mate. You're so close."

I nod my head, whimpering and panting into his mouth before sealing my lips over his. My nails bite into his shoulders, my back bows off the bed, and my thighs tighten around his hips as I come. Hard. It feels like my chest is being ripped open as I scream for him to keep going, again, harder, deeper, more, more, more.

I'm expecting him to follow me over the edge, but he just keeps hammering into me until I'm completely spent. I don't have any time to recover before he pulls out, grips my hips, and flips me over on my stomach, positioning me on all fours and thrusting back inside.

"Jesus, so tight," he grits out.

I can't even breathe; he's so deep inside of me, stroking his thick cock in and out and taking what he needs from me. I'm sore and swollen, and still, I want more. I begin rocking back into him, making him growl and tighten his grip on my hips.

"Yes, Hudson, I love it like this," I moan.

"Goddamn, baby, I'll give this to you every single day if it makes you happy."

I can't speak, so I nod my head and whimper out some sort of response. Hudson must like it because he picks up his speed, using his strong arms to bounce me off his cock. My fingers curl into the sheets as I throw my head back and let out a broken cry.

A storm swirls deep in my core, the pressure gathering and threatening to consume me, body and soul. Hudson reaches around me and rubs furious circles over my clit, grinding his dick against me and filling me up completely. My orgasm flashes through me like lightning piercing through the sky. The storm clouds break open, raining down pleasure and washing me out to sea. I'm drowning in ecstasy when I hear Hudson's thunderous roar. He empties himself deep inside my pussy, his cock twitching and filling me up with so much cum it spills out of me.

He collapses on top of me, pressing my body into the mattress. I love feeling his weight on top of me, like he's anchoring me right here, keeping me in the moment. My mate brushes his lips over my mark, sending tremors down my spine.

Eventually, Hudson rolls over onto his back, getting settled before he drags me over his chest and tucks me into his side.

"Holy fuck," Hudson says in astonishment.

I grin. "Yeah. Holy fuck."

Hudson tips his chin down to look at me, shock and amusement dancing in his brilliant blue eyes. "We should have done that months ago."

"Mmhmm," I agree, nodding into his chest and snuggling up closer to him. Hudson reaches out for the blankets and pulls them over us.

"We'll clean up later, mate. Just rest for now."

I nod, letting the bliss of this moment wash over me. Hudson glides his fingertips up and down my spine in calming strokes, the steady beat of his heart lulling me to sleep.

Somewhere in the back of my mind, I know we have more to talk about. But right here, right now? This is everything. My mate and I will figure everything else out.

TEN

Hudson

ISLA STIRS in my arms and lets out a little contented sigh. It's just after seven-thirty in the morning, but I've been up for hours just watching her sleep. Obsessive, I know, but I'm way past caring at this point.

She's so fucking beautiful. Has it really only been two days since she showed up at my home to quit? Isla was a snarky thorn in my side, and now she's my whole goddamn world.

Isla mumbles something in her sleep, which makes me smile. It's still a new thing for me, this whole smiling business. I can't say I don't like it. At least around her.

I slide the covers off us and kiss my way down Isla's incredible body. I settle between her legs and part them, looking at her perfect little pussy. I suppress a groan when I see she's already wet for me. My dirty little mate. I flatten my tongue and drag it up her delicious cunt, sucking on her clit when I get to the top.

Isla moans softly, though I can tell she's still sleeping. I continue sucking on her folds, licking up every inch of her sweet pussy, and finally, I spear my tongue in her entrance.

This gets her attention.

"Hudson? Oh... Ohmygod," she gasps.

I feel her hands on my head, tugging at my hair and pushing me closer. I chuckle at her eagerness, which makes her moan again. I'm suffocating on her intoxicating pussy, and there's nowhere else I'd rather be.

When I have to lift my head up for air, I see Isla's beautiful blue eyes staring down at me in awe and lust. I place one hand between her round, firm breasts and slide it down her body. She arches her back at my touch, which thrusts her wet, hot cunt into my face. Taking the hint, I get back to work, alternating fast and slow strokes, hard and soft strokes, until Isla is whimpering and writhing at the tip of my tongue.

"I need to come," she whines. "I need it so bad," she cries out, bucking her hips and riding my face.

I growl and bite down on her clit, causing her to convulse and soak my face with her release. I drink down her essence and place sloppy kisses up her body until I take her mouth. Isla kisses me right back and then licks her cream off my chin.

"You like how you taste?"

"Mmhmm..." she says, all breathy and sexy as fuck, before she bites my lip and kisses me again.

When we break apart, I see her eyes glossed over, her pupils blown wide with lust. She gets a wicked grin on her face that makes my cock twitch. Isla buries her face in my neck and nips my skin, causing me to groan.

"Your turn," she whispers before shoving me off of her with a surprising force.

Before I can even register her words, Isla straddles me and kisses the fuck out of me. She gets me all worked up and then rips her mouth away from mine, making me growl in frustration. Isla just smiles and then kisses her way down my chest, scooting down my body, kissing my abs, lower, lower, till she's between my legs, kissing the tip of my swollen cock.

"Holy fuck," I hiss, gritting my teeth together.

She hesitates for a second, biting her bottom lip as she studies my thickness. Goddamn, the way she's staring at my dick has me leaking precum. This must snap her out of her insecurities because the next thing I know, she's licking up the little liquid pearl and then putting her mouth around me.

"Jesus, mate," I grunt. She's hardly even done anything yet, and I'm already on edge. I fist the sheets, resisting the urge to grab her head and fuck her mouth.

Isla smiles with my dick in her mouth, which is ridiculously sweet and sexy and perfectly Isla. She bobs her head up and down, taking in a little more of me each time. Then she fucking shoves her face down on me until I hit the back of her throat. She gags around my cock, and my hand finds the back of her head. It takes every single ounce of control I have not to shove her down even more so she's deep-throating me. Instead, I weave my fingers in her hair and tug her back a bit.

"Relax, baby. You're so beautiful, giving me pleasure like this. Breathe, mate."

She breathes through her nose and starts sucking on me again, massaging the underside of my cock with her tongue.

"That's it, Isla, fuck, that's so fucking it," I groan.

She scrapes her nails over my balls, making me tighten my grip on her hair and buck my hips. I worry that I am too rough, but then she fucking moans and takes me deeper.

"So good, baby, so fucking good."

Isla is perfect; already a pro at reading my body and responding. She cups my balls and sucks me into the back of her throat again, swallowing around the head of my cock.

"I'm close, shit, Isla..."

Fuck, I want to come down her throat so badly, but I want to be inside of her little cunt more. I pull on her hair, popping her off of my dick. She pouts, which makes me chuckle.

"Need inside that little pussy of yours," I say by way of explanation. She licks her lips and nods as she climbs up my body and straddles me. "You want to ride me, dirty girl?"

She nods and bites her lip, so damn sexy and eager.

I slide my hands up her legs and grip her hips, holding her above my aching cock.

"I want that too, mate," I growl. Isla nods again, then drops herself down on me in one swift motion, making us both cry out. "Take it slow, sweetheart; you have to be sore from last night."

"I'm okay; I just want you so much. Is that bad? I feel like I'm going crazy."

I reach out and tuck some hair behind her ear, sliding my hand around to the back of her neck so I can pull her down for a kiss.

"It's not bad. Fuck, I want you too, so much. I'm glad I'm not the only one going crazy."

I slide my hands down her back and grip her ass, helping her grind down on me until she finds what feels good. Isla braces herself with a hand on either side of my head, placing her delicious tits right in my face. I suck on her breasts and bite her nipples while Isla rolls her hips and fucks me with everything she has.

"Hudson! Oh fuck..."

I groan as I tighten my hold on her curves, pushing and pulling as we find our perfect rhythm. Isla tenses and buries her head in my neck as her entire body goes still. Then, all at once, she loses control, her body spasming around me. She bites my neck and fucking gushes all over me, her release dripping down my balls.

I grab her ass, pull her cheeks apart, and fuck up into her, grunting each time I hit home. Isla cries out, and a fresh wave of wetness coats me as she comes again, her pussy choking the life out of my dick.

With a roar, I bite her mark and shoot my load deep inside her, filling her so full it leaks out of her pussy. The bed is a mess, sloppy with our combined orgasms, which only makes everything that much hotter.

Isla takes a shuddering breath and then goes limp in my arms, her little heart beating so fast in her chest. I wrap my arms around her and hold her close as we both come back to earth.

We don't say anything for a while. I stroke her back with one hand while the other grips her ass possessively, holding her close to me.

I don't want to ever move from this position, but I meant what I said earlier. Isla can't stay here with the Twisted Oak pack. It's too dangerous. If anything ever happened to her...

My bear growls, and I rub the heel of my hand over my chest, calming him down.

"Is everything okay?" Isla asks, popping her head up from where it was tucked into my shoulder.

"Yeah," I rasp, starting to sit up. Looking over at the clock on the nightstand, I frown when I see it's already after ten. As much as I want to keep Isla all wrapped up in my bed, the longer she stays here, the more at risk she is.

Some part of me knows I'm being paranoid, but I can't help it. The pack members here are notoriously rowdy, unpredictable, and prone to violence. I just found my mate; there's no way I'm going to put her in danger by asking her to stay here with me. We'll figure something out. I can visit all the time, and I'll make sure my internet is always strong so we can do video calls too.

"Are you sure?" Isla asks, pulling me out of my racing thoughts. "Because you look like you're trying to do trigonometry in your head or something. I wouldn't worry too much about it. You're the artist, remember? Math isn't really your thing."

She gives me her signature sweet and sassy grin, and I do my best to return it even though there's a lead weight in my stomach.

"It's getting to be kind of late in the morning," I announce as I climb out of bed. Throwing on a pair of sweatpants, I make my way to the front window, peering out of the curtains. Two wolf shifters are racing across the clearing, nipping at each others' heels as they sprint toward the tree line. I know those two fuckers, Mike and Jared, and they're never up to anything good. Isla needs to get in her car and forget this town ever existed. "You should probably head back to your apartment."

My words are met with silence, and I turn to face Isla. She's staring at me with a blank look in her eyes. I wonder if she heard me or not, so I try again.

"You'll probably want to get back home soon, right? Get a change of clothes and all that." I don't mean to be rude, but my adrenaline has spiked now that I know Mike and Jared are around. They might scent her out as a human and try to mess with her just because they can. I'd have to rip their throats out for threatening my mate, and then I really would be the monster everyone thinks I am.

No, it's best that Isla leaves now, and we can talk about what our future will look like once she's in the safety of her own town and her own apartment. It's the only way I can think of to make this work. I just hope she understands.

"Right," she says softly. I furrow my brow at her tone, but then she says it again. "Right. Of course." This time, her voice is clipped, her tone cold enough to give me frostbite.

"Isla…" I start, but what do I say? I don't want to have this conversation right now. It would take too much time, and right now, my priority is getting my mate to safety.

"I get it. No need to keep up the pretense," she spits out.

"Pretense?" *What the hell is she talking about?*

Instead of answering, she slips out of bed and throws her old clothes on before stomping to the kitchen counter and grabbing her purse. Before I even know what's happening, my mate is storming out the door, leaving me gaping after her. I follow her out to the porch, still confused as fuck.

"Are you upset?" I ask, running a hand through my messy morning hair.

Isla throws open her car door, then turns to face me.

"Upset? *Upset?!*" she screeches.

"Shh," I warn her, my eyes darting toward the forest to make sure Mike and Jared didn't hear.

"Bold move to be shushing me as you're kicking me out of your house. I'm not *upset*, Hudson. I'm pissed at myself for falling for your whole *fated mates* line. God, I'm an idiot," she says, each word puncturing my heart.

"What? You don't understand, Isla. That's not—"

"No need to explain any further," she grits out, cutting me off. "I get it."

She slams her car door and starts the engine, peeling out of my gravel driveway in a huff. Dust and rocks kick back behind her car, and as confused as I am, relief washes over me now that she's out of harm's way.

It's only when I get back inside that I piece together what just happened.

Pacing in front of the window, I replay our conversation over and over. She thinks I kicked her out, which I guess, technically, I did. But it was for her own good. Doesn't she get that?

No, I suppose not. We didn't spend a lot of time talking about the Twisted Oak pack. I told her that it's a pack full of loners and monsters, but I never told her how much danger she would be in if anyone found out I had a human mate.

"Goddamnit," I growl, hating myself for not thinking of how it would sound for me to send her on her way after the time we spent together.

The rest of our conversation filters through my mind. She called herself an idiot for falling for me. She really thinks I lied about fated mates? Why?

To get in her pants, stupid, my bear points out.

No. She can't truly think I was... using her for sex. Even thinking the words makes me sick to my stomach. Never in a million years would that have crossed my mind. It hurts more than I can express that Isla thinks that little of me, but I can't blame her. I suck at communicating, let alone talking about this kind of shit with the most important person in my life.

That's no excuse, though. I need to try harder. I need to find a way to make her trust me again, at least enough to explain that I'd never reject her.

Fuck. How did I screw this up so badly? Maybe I really don't deserve to have a mate, just like I always thought. Still, I have to fight for her. If she doesn't want to be with me, I'll have to deal with that. I can't leave it like this, though. I can't have her thinking I don't want her or that last night wasn't the greatest experience of my life.

You've got your work cut out for you, my bear says.

I know. Thanks for the vote of confidence, buddy.

ELEVEN

Isla

I KNEW *I shouldn't have trusted him,* I think to myself for
the ten thousandth time these last few days. Pulling the
fleece blanket tighter around my shoulders, I relax back into
the couch with my laptop open, prepared for another day of
job searching.

I only make it to the second listing before my mind
wanders back to Hudson. I should have listened to my gut
instead of chasing after such an obviously emotionally
unavailable man.

I never thought I'd be one of those girls who fell face-
first into a relationship only to end up being used. Now
look at me. I'm back in my apartment, nursing a broken
heart.

I've spent the last three days applying for every job I
can find. So far, I've had two phone interviews, but I kind of
bombed them. Okay, not kind of. I was a total space cadet
the entire time and could hardly focus enough to answer

basic questions. I would honestly be shocked if I got a call back about either of them.

Hudson has been trying to call and email me every single day, multiple times a day since I left Twisted Oak, but I've been ignoring his attempts to talk. What could he possibly say to make up for the way he treated me? I'm just too hurt and pissed off at him to have any sort of meaningful conversation right now. I need to process everything and figure out what I want. Then I can speak with him. Or not.

The hard part is figuring out what I want. Even through my anger and heartache, my mind keeps circling back to the raw, genuine moments we shared. Like when Hudson told me about his family, about how lost and lonely he's been. Was that all an act?

It all seemed so simple to me a few days ago, but now that I've been with Hudson, now that I've gotten to know him and he's bitten me... Well, things are more complicated than ever.

"I'm headed out to work. Do you need anything?" Hattie asks me cautiously as she peers into the living room.

Neither of us has ever had our hearts broken, and I can tell Hattie doesn't know how to navigate mine. She's been trying to stay by my side, to distract me when she can and let me cry or rant when she can't. I don't know what I would do without her.

"No, I'm okay."

"Are you sure? I can call out again," she offers.

It's tempting, but I know that we need the money right now.

"I'll be okay," I promise her, and she smiles slightly.

"Okay, I'll be back later. Call me if you need anything," she says as she heads for the door.

"Will do."

She leaves, and I shove my laptop aside, laying back on the couch and staring up at the ceiling as I try to figure out what my next move should be.

I don't know how long I lay there, trying to sort through my feelings, when there's a knock at the door. I frown, wondering who that could be, when they knock again, harder this time.

"Jeez, hold onto your horses," I mumble as I push to my feet. I pause briefly, taking inventory of my ratty pajamas, messy hair, and generally slovenly appearance. Oh well. Who do I have to impress anyway?

I pull the door open, expecting it to be our landlord or maybe someone trying to sell us something. Instead, I'm greeted by Hudson's scowling face.

"No," I snarl, trying to slam the door closed in his face, but he's faster.

He jams his foot into the doorframe, his big hand wrapping around the door as he pushes it open.

"Knock it off," he snaps at me, and I back up as he approaches.

He slams the front door closed behind him, and I cross my arms over my chest.

"Get out. I don't want to see you right now. Maybe ever."

"You can't just disappear like that!" he says, looking completely unhinged.

"Are you seriously yelling at me right now? After the way you treated me?"

"Fuck, Isla, I've been losing my goddamn mind."

"That's not an answer to my question," I continue, jutting my chin out in defiance.

He doesn't say anything as his eyes roam up and down my body. It's not a lustful gaze, more like he's taking inventory and making sure I'm not hurt in any way. It's not sweet. At least, that's what I'm telling myself.

The more I study Hudson's face, the more I see just how rattled he is. There are dark bags under his eyes and he looks pale. Fury shines bright in his eyes, but it's not just anger swirling in their depths. Worry and sadness are also there.

Don't let it sway you. He kicked you out! He doesn't want you!

I straighten my spine, tightening my hands into fists and setting my jaw as I stare him down.

"I didn't disappear. I left. Like you ordered me to," I remind him.

"I've been calling! I've been emailing and trying to contact you for the last few days, and you've been ignoring me. I thought something happened to you. Something awful. I've been so worried, you have no idea," he blurts out in a frenzy.

"You were worried? Then why the heck did you push me away? Why even bite me and supposedly make me your mate if you were just going to abandon me in the end?"

"I'm not abandoning you. I'm trying to keep you safe," he argues.

"You have a really funny way of showing it. Sleeping with me, then sending me on my way once you got what you wanted. Besides, I can take care of myself."

"Not from everything. It's my job as your mate to keep you safe. Isla, that morning I told you to go home, I saw two Twisted Oak pack members circling in the woods. They could have scented you and..."

"And what? What's the real reason you don't want me to stay with you?

"Like I said, your safety always comes first. It's not just about the other pack members. It's about..."

Hudson bows his head and rubs the back of his neck before looking at me once more. I see torment and self-hatred bubbling to the surface, and even though I'm still frustrated and confused, I can't stand to see this man in so much pain.

"It's about you," I say softly, finishing his thought for him.

"I have to protect you," he repeats, his tone begging me to believe him.

"Even from yourself." Those words hang between us, and I straighten my shoulders. "That's what you mean, right?" I challenge him, and he swallows hard.

"Yes," he finally admits.

"You're not a monster, though." I've already told him as much, but I realize it will take more than that to undo a lifetime of people saying the opposite.

My words spark something to life in Hudson, and his eyes burn with equal parts exasperation and anger. "Tell that to everyone who thinks I murdered my family!"

"I'm not one of them!" I shout right back. "I never believed that. Anyone who really knows you wouldn't believe that!"

"It doesn't..." he doesn't finish that sentence, so I do it for him.

"It doesn't matter? Is that what you were going to say? What I think *doesn't matter?*"

"It does!"

"Then what is all of this? Why did you bite me? Why did you claim me?"

"Because you're my mate."

"Is that even real? Or just a line you use on anyone stupid enough to believe it?"

"Yes! Fated mates are sacred. They are special and to be honored above all else. I wouldn't lie about that, and I wouldn't lie to you, period. You're my mate. I know you feel it too. That's why we're so fucking miserable without each other. It hurts being away from you."

"And what if I don't want to be your mate anymore?"

"Isla," he starts, taking a panicked step toward me.

"I want a partner. I want someone who wants to be by my side. I want to fall asleep next to my husband and wake up to his face. I don't want to be alone and in a relationship," I tell him.

I don't know why it took me so long to realize that. Maybe I knew deep down that's what I wanted, but I didn't want to admit it because it meant leaving Hudson.

"Isla, I..." he starts, but I shake my head.

"Am I what you want? Honestly? Are you happy living away from me?"

"No," he admits, and the word sounds dragged out of him.

"Then why are you doing this to both of us? Why don't you want to be happy? Why don't you want to make me happy?"

"I do," he insists, and I shake my head.

"Then you wouldn't be pushing me away. You would be moving away from Twisted Oak."

I can see the war raging inside of him at my words. He wants to do anything to make me happy and keep me as his mate, but he's been thinking that he deserves to live in that nightmare town for so long. It's hard for him to see the light.

"I wouldn't love you if you were a monster, Hudson," I say quietly, and his eyes widen.

"You love me?" he asks.

He looks unbearably vulnerable at this moment, and that's when I see it. The power I hold. Hudson has given me his heart and soul, and he's terrified I'm going to crush them.

"Of course, I love you," I murmur, taking a step toward him. I notice for the first time that Hudson's muscles are so tense he's shaking. I may not understand everything about him yet, but I know he's telling me the truth. He wants to protect me. I'll just need to show him that he doesn't need to protect me from him. "I wouldn't have slept with you or let you bite me if I didn't love you. What kind of girl do you think I am?" I say with a tiny smirk, hoping to lighten the mood.

Hudson swallows hard, unshed tears in his intense eyes. "Can you... can you say it again?" he asks.

Tears spring to my eyes at his request, and I sway closer to him, needing to be nearer. "I love you, Hudson," I tell him again. "And you're not a monster. You never were. I love you."

He closes the distance between us, and his hands cup my face.

"I love you too. God, it feels so weird to say that after so many years."

I nod, the tears falling down my cheeks as I stare up at him.

"I've been alone for so long, but I don't want that anymore. I want to have a family. I want to have you. I want to keep you and be whatever you need. Tell me how to love you, and I swear I'll do it."

I nod again, and he smiles down at me, his thumbs smoothing over my cheekbones and wiping away the last of my tears.

"I love you, Isla. I'll move for you. I'll do anything for you."

"The apartment is small, but you can move in here. I'm not sure where you would do your art, though."

"Thanks for the offer, but I actually think I know a better place than either of ours. It's a small town a little north of here. I have a few shifter friends who just moved there with their human mates, and they love it. We could go check it out," he offers.

"Hattie has to like it too," I'm quick to interject. "I won't move without her."

"Of course," he says right away, and I smile.

"I missed you," I admit, and he smiles.

"I was going crazy, losing my mind missing you."

They are the last words either of us say before our lips fuse together. Hudson dives into my mouth, taking control of the kiss as his hands roam up and down my curves. I cling to my muscled, sexy beast, feeling complete for the first time in days.

"God, you're incredible," he murmurs into the side of my neck. "Smell so good. Taste so good. Fuck," Hudson grunts, sounding almost in pain. "Need you naked. Need to show you how much I love you."

"Yes," I manage to whisper, barely able to comprehend his words, just knowing I need him more than air.

The next thing I know, Hudson spins me around and grips my hips, pulling my back into his front. I moan softly when Hudson presses his lips to the side of my neck, kissing up and down and swirling his tongue over my mark. I feel his lips brush against the shell of my ear, the deep rumble of his voice vibrating through me.

"Put your hands on the back of the couch, Isla." I do as

he says, looking over my shoulder at him. "Just like that. Fuck, just like that."

He kneels down behind me, hooking his thumbs into the waistband of my leggings. Hudson peels them off, right along with my panties. I gasp as the cool air hits my soaking wet folds. My core clenches and I feel my arousal drip down my thighs.

Hudson grabs my ass in his large, capable hands, squeezing the soft flesh and then spreading me wide open for him. I widen my stance, wanting him to have more. To take more. To take it all. "Please," I whimper.

I feel so vulnerable, so exposed, and so, *so* needy. Hudson has barely touched me, yet my clit is throbbing almost painfully. A growl rumbles up from deep in his chest, and then I feel his lips and nose glide along my slit. I tremble at the featherlight touch, gasping when he breathes me in. Hudson buries his face into my cunt, licking me from top to bottom. I cry out and grip the couch, bracing myself as he teases my opening with the tip of his tongue.

Hudson's hands roam up and down my thighs, spreading me open as he devours me. I feel his tongue everywhere, gliding through my folds, playing with my bundle of nerves, darting in and out of my tight hole. I don't realize I'm holding my breath until Hudson wraps his lips around my clit and sucks. *Hard.* All of the air leaves my lungs, followed by a desperate, breathy moan.

I lower myself onto my forearms on the back of the couch, resting my head on my arm. It's all I can do to keep from collapsing. Every swipe of his tongue is followed by a low, strained grunt. He sounds like he can't get enough like he's gorging on me and doesn't want to come up for air. That thought has me pressing back against him, offering him everything he wants.

"Fuck," he growls, gasping for air. Hudson dives back in, licking me, sucking me, scraping his teeth along my sensitive folds and swollen clit.

My legs start shaking uncontrollably as every muscle in my body tenses. I'm so close. My stomach clenches, my heart pounds, and my joints lock up. I hold my breath, preparing for the pleasure to come.

I just need one more swipe of his tongue, one more, so close... one more...

Hudson pulls back, making me whimper in frustration. He chuckles darkly; then I feel the sting of his hand as he spanks me. I gasp in shock, then cry out in pleasure as he does it again on the other side. I don't have time to wonder why that feels so damn good before Hudson puts his mouth on me once more.

He licks me in fierce, fast strokes, winding me up, higher, higher, higher...

"Oh god," I whisper. "Oh god, oh god, ohmygod..."

My orgasm floods through me, drowning me in ecstasy. I keep coming, wave after wave of endless bliss, overwhelming every single one of my senses. Hudson swallows down my release, dipping his tongue inside my entrance like he can't get enough. All I can do is tremble and let out breathy, pained little whimpers.

TWELVE

Hudson

"AGAIN," I growl into her tight, hot cunt.

Isla moans as her hips buck, grinding herself back against my mouth. I grab her hips and pull her even closer until I'm suffocating inside her sweet heat. I lick her clit again and again until my tongue is numb. She sucks in a huge breath and then cries out her climax so beautifully for me.

Before she has a chance to recover, I scoop her up in my arms and lay her down on the couch, crawling up her body and kissing her hard and deep. She takes everything I give her, moaning at her taste in my mouth.

Not wasting any more time, I rip her flimsy t-shirt down the middle, loving the fact that she's not wearing a bra. Isla giggles at first but then moans as I suck one tit into my mouth. She bows her back off the couch, thrusting her chest further into me. I kiss and lick my way to her other breast and give it the same attention.

I leave her briefly, only to unbuckle my belt and pull off my jeans and underwear. I grab one of her ankles and place it over the back of the couch while the other one rests on my shoulder, spreading her wide open for me. Looking down at this stunning woman, chest heaving, pussy dripping, eyes fogged over with lust, I can't help but groan.

"So fucking beautiful. God, you're perfect, Isla."

I line myself up and enter her tight little channel in one long thrust. I growl, just feeling her silky heat against my aching cock. Isla throws her head back and claws at the couch cushions. She gushes for me, making it easy to slide in and out of her. I pick up my pace, needing her to come again, needing to show her how much I love her, how I'm never leaving her.

"Mine," I grunt as I piston in and out of her. "My mate."

"Y-yours, oh, fuck, fuck, Hudson, I can't hold on…"

"Let go, Isla. I love watching you come. I love hearing you come. I love feeling you come all around me."

Her orgasm slams into her, causing her body to shake and convulse beneath me. I fuck her through her orgasm as she whimpers and writhes. I can't hold off much longer, but I don't want this to end. I want to be inside of my mate forever.

I pull out of her as she moans, snapping her eyes open and searing me with her lustful gaze. Standing up, I pull her into me and spin her around, guiding her to lean over the arm of the couch. I grab her hair and guide her to lean forward onto her elbows. I press my cock against her soaking wet pussy, her previous releases dripping down her thighs. I tease her as I wait for the exact, right moment.

"Hudson, please, please get inside of me."

"I'll always give you what you need, mate."

I tease her a little longer, rubbing my cock up and down

her slit. When she starts shaking and whimpering, I slam my thick dick deep inside her, triggering another orgasm. I roar with pride over how much pleasure I can give my woman and how well she takes all of my many inches.

My hips snap as I buck and thrust, my heavy balls slapping her pussy. Every time we join together, we make the most obscene and glorious wet-smacking sounds. I can't tell if she's having one long orgasm or if she's had five more, but her pussy has been squeezing and snapping around me the entire time. I loop my arm around her waist, holding her up just as she starts to collapse. I give one more hard thrust before exploding inside of her.

My teeth find her mark as I bite down, my orgasm barrelling through me while I suck on her sensitive skin. It's so intense, so fucking everything. I keep emptying into her, coming harder than I ever have. Each rope of cum feels like it's taking a part of my very soul, draining me and pouring more of me into her. I'll give her everything. There is no me without her.

Finally, fucking *finally*, I'm completely spent. I curl my body over hers, covering her back with my front as I place a gentle kiss over her mark, loving the salty taste of her sweat.

Isla is shaking in my arms, panting and sweating, and well-fucked.

"You okay, mate?" I whisper into her ear.

"I... I'm...," she breathes out. "S-so good. Can't feel my legs."

I chuckle and then stand up, pulling out of her swollen, soaked pussy. Spinning her around again, I scoop Isla up into my arms. She's a fucking rag doll, and I chuckle again, kissing her forehead before collapsing on the couch with her in my lap.

She curls up into my chest and rests her head in the crook of my neck.

"I love you," I whisper, smoothing my hand up and down her bare back.

"Love you, too, mate," she says back, nuzzling further into my side.

After a few moments of silence, Isla pops her head up, a mischievous little grin lighting up her face. "Does this mean I get to keep my job?"

I chuckle, pressing a kiss to her forehead. "Yeah, if you think you can deal with your un-*bear*-able boss."

Isla groans, playfully smacking me in the chest. "I don't know. Are you going to make awful bear puns from now on?"

"You'll *bear*-ly notice," I counter, loving the fire in her eyes.

She opens her mouth, a sassy comment on the tip of her tongue, but I kiss the breath from her lungs before she gets a chance to say anything. I have a feeling I'll be using this tactic a lot in our future. I also have a feeling my mate won't mind.

THIRTEEN

Isla

"YOUR NEW SUPPLIES CAME IN," I tell my husband, carrying the box that just came in the mail into Hudson's art studio.

"You shouldn't be carrying that!" He snaps, rushing over to take the box out of my hands.

"It's not that heavy," I tell him, and he shakes his head.

"You're carrying enough already," he says, his hand falling to my swollen stomach.

I'm pregnant with our second child, and he's going to be big, just like his daddy. Our first son, Rowan, was big, too, and you think that Hudson would be used to it, but he's just as overprotective this pregnancy as he was with the last.

"Why don't you sit down?" Hudson suggests as he practically lowers me into the comfy armchair he keeps in his studio just for me.

"Are you almost done with this masterpiece?" I ask him, nodding over to the sculpture in the center of the room.

"Almost. I should have it ready to be shipped tomorrow."

I smile as Hudson hovers over me.

"You can go back to work. I was about to head inside and start making dinner. Rowan should be up from his nap soon."

"I'll come in and help you. This can wait."

I smile. I love that about Hudson. Rowan and I, we always come first for him. He's the best dad to our son, and he's the best partner and husband to me.

Hudson and I moved to the North Star pack a month after we were mated. We took Hattie with us, but she moved out pretty quickly when she found her own mates. Now, she lives right down the road with them. We still see each other every day and have play dates with our kids. We both finally have the family that we always wanted.

I'm still working as Hudson's assistant, though now I'm much happier. The pay is better, and the benefits can't be beat. I smile to myself as I remember some of the benefits that Hudson and I had last night.

As if he can read my mind, his eyes darken, and I see him breathing in deeply. I know that he must be able to smell my arousal.

Good.

Hudson helps me out of the chair and keeps my hand in his as we exit the studio and head over to the house. We live in a bungalow-style place on the edge of a meadow. Hudson says that the scenery inspires him, and Rowan and I love to play and read in the meadow every afternoon.

"Are you going out for a run tonight?" I ask him.

He likes to let his bear out to run and explore our new home at least once a week. Usually, that happens to fall on a Tuesday or Wednesday, but with the full moon tonight, I doubt that he'll have running on his mind.

"Are you kidding me? My bear and I have a little something more exciting than that in mind," he says, giving me a wink.

I grin, pressing my body against his as we head inside.

"Naughty girl," he whispers, and I smirk.

"I don't know what you mean," I lie.

"You're a little tease, and you know it," he growls at me with a grin.

"How do you know that I'm teasing? Rowan will be asleep for at least another twenty minutes."

His eyes spark with heat, and the next thing I know, he's swooping me up off my feet and taking the steps two at a time up to our room.

"Shh!" I shush him. "We can't wake Rowan."

"Face down for you it is then," he says cockily, and I giggle as he sets me on the bed and reaches for the hem of my dress. "No panties? Man, I'm one lucky bastard."

He lifts my dress off my body, then proceeds to touch me everywhere, his hands mapping me out and making me quiver in anticipation. Hudson starts by gliding his fingers down my shoulders, then over my breasts, stopping briefly to tweak my nipples. Lower, lower, lower, his hands roam until they grasp my thighs and spread me wide open.

Hudson dips two fingers into my slit, groaning when he feels how wet I am. He rubs my clit and plunges two fingers into my pulsing, wet hole while I writhe beneath him. Hudson withdraws his fingers and wipes my honey over my lips before kissing it off. I swear I almost come from that alone.

I wiggle my hips, trying to get him where I need him most. Hudson takes the hint, ridding himself of his clothing in record time. My mate crawls on top of me, positioning his cock at my entrance. He surges forward, hitting the end of me in one long thrust.

"Mate," he groans, holding himself still inside of me. "You feel so damn good."

I whimper and nod my head in agreement. Hudson claims my mouth again, sucking on my tongue while pulling out and setting a frantic pace.

My legs tighten around his hips, and my hands grip the tight muscles in his back. I hang on to this powerful beast as he fucks me with rough strokes, imprinting himself on me, in me, for all of time. No one will ever make me feel this way. No one but my Hudson. My mate.

I feel his mouth on my neck, his teeth scraping along my mark while his thumb circles my clit. Gasping for air, my spine arches, lifting me off the bed as I dig my nails into his back. My orgasm is right there, so close, my muscles stretch as my body reaches out for it...

Hudson pinches my clit, and I explode, crying out his name as my pussy spasms around him, trying to suck him in deeper.

"Jesus, you feel incredible, coming around my cock like a good girl. Let's see if I can get you to do it again."

With that, Hudson stands up and pulls me with him, readjusting our position. He sits down on the edge of the bed and guides me to straddle him. I give my mate a devious look and climb onto his lap, slowly, slowly easing my way down his thick dick.

"God, Isla..." he groans as he thrusts up, closing the distance between us. "Ready for more?"

I nod and sink my teeth into the firm flesh of his shoulder, earning me the sexy growl of a man barely able to control himself. Good. I don't want him to. "Fuck me, Hudson," I moan into his ear before pulling his earlobe between my teeth.

That's all the permission he needs.

Hudson grabs my ass with both hands, spreads it wide, and thrusts into me, fucking me so deep, so rough. I throw my head back and gasp as he fucks the air right out of my lungs, the scream out of my throat, my soul out of my body.

I bounce up and down on his cock, my pussy raw and sore and so sensitive but ready to take another beating. Hudson looks between us, where we're joined, and groans, almost sounding like he's in pain.

"Love watching you take all of me like a good girl. This pussy is mine, fucking *mine*." He tilts my hips slightly and hammers into my G-spot, the intense pleasure wracking my body with every stroke.

It hits me like lightning. The orgasm starts in my spine and then shoots down to my pussy, wet and throbbing between my legs. I come all over his fat cock, unable to stop as he spreads me wider and fucks me harder. I take all of him and come again, letting it spread all over his cock as he growls his pleasure, biting my lips and spanking my ass, tearing me in two with each thrust.

"Oh god," I gasp, pushing down on his length and holding myself there. My legs quiver, and I feel weak. I whimper in his arms.

"I've got you, Isla. Let go for me, baby; let it happen."

"Hudson... I can't... I don't..."

"Come for me, mate. One more time. Come so fucking hard."

Hudson slams into me one last time, breaking me wide open and releasing the ball of pressure built up deep inside of me. I gush for him as I convulse violently. My pussy keeps knotting around Hudson's cock, again and again, leaking more juices between us and making a mess of the sheets.

"Jesus, you're squirting all over me, baby, fuck, fuck, fuck..." Hudson barely manages to contain his roar as he succumbs to his orgasm, every muscle tensing and releasing in jerky motions.

I go limp in his arms, my body numb and devoid of strength. Hudson holds me tightly and thrusts into me once, twice, three times before collapsing backward on the bed.

When I open my eyes again, Hudson and I are lying in bed on our sides, facing each other. Hudson is holding me close and tracing a line from my shoulder down to my hip and back again.

"Mate," Hudson says as we both catch our breath, and I grin up at him.

"I know. I love you too."

He smiles down at me, and we both laugh when the sound of Rowan waking up in his room reaches us.

"Perfect timing. I'll get him. You rest for a bit."

"Okay. I have a feeling that I'm going to need my strength tonight," I tell him, rolling onto my side in the bed.

He laughs, giving me a devilish smirk as he climbs out of bed to get dressed.

"Oh, you definitely will," he promises.

Want to read Isla's story? Check out her love story with Alex, Max, and Robin here!

WANT A FREE BOOK?

Want a free copy of Wolf Lover? It's a steamy, scarred military hero, curvy girl romance! Check it out today here!

CONNECT WITH ME!

If you enjoyed this story, please consider leaving a review on Amazon or any other reader site or blog that you like. Don't forget to recommend it to your other reader friends.

If you want to chat with me, please consider joining my VIP list or connecting with me on one of my Social Media platforms. I love talking with each of my readers. Links below!

Website

Aspen Ridge Pack: Shifter M.D.

Bitten By The Doctor

Bound To The Doctor

Fated To The Doctor

Marked By The Doctor

Aspen Ridge Pack: Loners

The Grizzlies Captive Mate